By Chris Baugh

Cover design by Steven Lawver

This book is a work of fiction. Names, characters, places and incidents are the product of the author's imagination. Any resemblance to actual events, locations or people, living or dead, is coincidental.

Copyright © 2003 Chris Baugh

All rights reserved. No part of this book may be reproduced in any form or by any electronic or mechanical means, including information storage and retrieval systems, without permission in writing from the author, except by a reviewer who may quote brief passages in a review.

American International Publishing
4008 Enterprise Court
Martinez, Georgia 30907

CHAPTER 1: THE ORB

"*Hahaha!* Would you look at that? Oh man! That semi-auto? Yeah right!"

"'Look at me! I'm a Starship Trooper! I'm fighting giant spiders with an M-16! Isn't this leather just so stylish? *Ouch!* It—certainly,'" he said as his voice got weaker and his words further apart, in such a way to make him sound like he was dying "'isn't – strong.' Man, what were those idiots thinking?"

"Hey, it's not their fault they didn't know anything at all!"

"Oh, well I guess your right. Poor souls, trapped in the Dark Age," John said to his roommates. John Smith was just a freshman in college on the International Space Station.

"So, Rich, when do you go to class?" John asked Richard, one of his four roommates.

"Well, um, I think its 0900 SST." Standard Space Time was used in space, everywhere in space. It was measured on a scale from 0000 hours to 2359 hours (midnight to 11:59).

"Lucky! I've got to go at 0800!" Suddenly, the intercom that they were so accustomed to hearing came on.

"Anyone majoring in Nuclear Chemistry, please report to your classroom shuttle at this time. Thank you."

John took his cue. "That's me . . . Do they realize how many hours of sleep I get with class this early?"

"Well, I bet they don't assume you stay up until four-hundred hours every night," another roommate, Chris, said as he stifled a laugh.

"Man! I mean, four hours of sleep before my first class? These people are insane! Even if I got to sleep at midnight, I've got my hardest class first!"

"Good morning, Mr. Smith! On your way to Chem class I assume? I would hate to see you late again." A passing teacher commented. He was John's Math teacher.

"Yes, sir! Of course I'm on my way! I'll see you at the end of the day I suppose," he responded, laughing under his breath.

The students were smart, but simply in college to have fun, like most of their colleagues. Chris was the unofficial leader. All of their pranks, and there were a lot of them, were usually engineered and executed, largely, by him. In the end, he got most of the blame pinned on him. "Man these teachers are hard! See you guys later!" He yawned. He then took the Space Station shuttle to his launch pad. For nuclear chemistry, they had to fly away from the station, in case . . .

"Coffee?" The man at the door asked John.

"Little Mikie? Still giving people the coffee? Man, and I thought you might have a job!" John made a habit of making fun of people less financially fortunate than himself, especially Mike, who was in his math class.

"Tall, black and sugar on the side?"

"Make it quick!"

"Always," Michael said. In a matter of seconds, John was at his launch pad.

"Sorry I'm late! The subway broke—

"No, it broke yesterday, if I recall correctly," the Chem teach said to John.

"Did it now? My mistake! You know, those hallways get so crowded in the morning!" His classmates began to laugh at John's morning regime of excuses.

"Did you blow up your homework again doing an experiment? Or did your roommate eat it again?" Once John had used the excuse that while attempting to record his results from an acid project, he made it too strong and it burned through the vile and then also dissolved his homework. He had also used the excuse that his friend had become hypnotized into thinking that he was on a strict diet of paper and ink, and therefore ate his homework before the hypnosis had worn off. He ended the excuse by saying that he barely escaped with his pen intact.

"Actually sir, this time, I sealed it in an indestructible, air-tight chamber so it wouldn't get damaged—"

"And you lost the case?" his teach asked dryly.

It All Started In Chem Class…

"Got it right here!" John then proceeded to remove from his pocket— to the surprise, astonishment, and all-out disbelief of his classmates— an airtight, seemingly indestructible, transparent case containing his homework on a sheet of plastic. People in this age used plastic, because you could use it in place of more than one-hundred sheets of paper. This was part of the EPA act of 2030. John handed in the homework, as did his classmates, jaws still wide. John was smart; he just lacked the care for homework. His opinion was: "I need that time to relax from the horrors of school. Making me do the schoolwork outside of school brings the horror back all too vividly! I need all the hours I'm not in school to purge the deep evil from me. That isn't right!" Unfortunately for him, Mr. Greeniferb didn't buy that.

"Class will now begin. Today, we will study how to create a new chemical compound. Does anyone know of two or more elements that form a chemical compound that is not already discovered?"

"Well, if you put arsenic, CO_2 and Nitro into a test tube, you get the best organic fart powder. Man, will that stink up a room!" His class lost it at that point. They were howling with laughter. It was a good thing they were actually in space, where there was a lack of gravity, or else they would have been on the floor. Then, as a form of payback for the fart powder joke, the teacher turned on the Gravity Field Projector, which caused the ship to spin, using gyroscopic momentum to create a gravitational environment.

"Now, on a more serious note," the teacher began again, a tear in his own eye from laughing so hard. "So, does anyone else have a chemical compound?" A girl John would have considered a nerd (who had braces, glasses, and acne like you would not believe) raised her hand. "Yes, Miss Thompson?"

"Well, I found, sir, that by combining the chemicals Hydrogen, Oxygen, Helium and Nitrogen one can create air similar to the air we breathe that can leave your voice permanently higher and also can help cure asthma," Courtney Thompson said shyly.

"Very good Miss Thompson. Asthma sufferers everywhere will be happy to know there is finally a cure. Excellent work!" The teacher was talking to his best student. One of John's other friends, who also enjoyed making smart remarks about the suck-ups and teacher pets said "Mr. Greeniferb, did you bring your dogs to school today? I could have sworn I smelled your pets around here!" Fortunately for him, Courtney did not understand the joke. Several of the other class members began to stifle laughs. That was about all that happened in Chem that day. Chem was, however, interrupted by a special guest speaker.

The shuttle came back to the Space Station. John, Chris, Richard, Jordan, and Bob all hooked up on the way to the meeting. John was the only one with a morning course on Monday. ("I need three full days to purge the evil!")

"So, does anyone have any idea what this is about?" Rich asked the group nonchalantly.

"I heard it was military recruiting blah blah blah," Chris replied as though he had woken up at 0200 hours and needed to go back to sleep.

"I heard it was one of those safety blah blah blah's," John said. As they walked to the floating Café Probe, the five friends decided to take a brief detour.

They randomly walked into a suspicious hallway. On occasion, they went looking for trouble but usually, "Trouble found me! I didn't mean to get jumped, it just sorta happened that way! What? How would I know that someone was standing on the ceiling?" This was one such excuse used by Rich for being late and involved in a fight before his starship engineering class. "Hey guys, do you see what I see?" Rich asked the group.

"Dude! That room is glowing!" Chris said, awestruck.

"And green, of all colors!" John said, quietly, in case there was anyone, or anything, which might not want them there.

"Let's go! This could be important! What if it's a bomb? We gotta check this out!" Chris whispered to all the others. Slowly, they walked forward and opened the door. They peered

It All Started In Chem Class...   5

inside. To their astonishment, all that was in there was a green orb, glowing and lighting up the whole room.

"Bob, get me a reading on that. Could be dangerous." Bob was majoring in exploration and explanation of the unknown. He had a device, as did all his classmates, that could read the energy of various things. This device could tell if something was dead, alive, or radioactive. Bob whipped out the device and held it up to the green orb.

"You're not gonna like this . . ."

"Alive?" Rich asked.

"Radioactive?" Chris said with concern.

"Neither," Bob replied with eyes wide as dinner plates.

"Then what's so bad?" Chris questioned with frustration in his voice.

"It's off the charts! I've never seen a reading like this before. They don't teach us this in EEU. I dunno if it's dangerous, superheated or what. This is unlike anything the EEU has dealt with before. I do have a standard issue, but I don't know if this would actually work. I don't know if this is alive— if it's a bomb! I don't know anything about it! Going to a teacher might not work. What can we do?" Bob was smart, but this time, he was at his wit's end.

"Well, we could try and take it, but that might look a little conspicuous, carrying a glowing green orb. We could go to a teach, but then, we would risk getting kicked out of school. Is there anything in a history book or anywhere that might give me an explanation? I don't know what to do!" Chris was frustrated. Suddenly, out of nowhere, the fifth roommate spoke up. Jordan, slightly more serious than his friends, gave sound, sagely advice.

"It is floating in midair. It appears as though it is suspended in a field of some sort. In truth, the reading might be coming from whatever sort of generator is suspending it and creating that field. Get a reading on the top and bottom," Jordan said quietly. Bob quickly did as he was told.

"Generators have a basic reading level; it's the orb that is off the charts. However, I think you may be right. Someone put this generator up, and amped a lot of power into this field. I'd be willing to bet that we aren't gonna be touching that thing any time soon," Bob said.

"Very nice generator. Top of the line. You're right about one thing. We sure aren't touching that field anytime soon. Whoa! I've never seen a generator with this much power in my life! This thing has more power than the generators on the Nuclear Chem Class Shuttle. This thing is a mechanical monster! They tell us in Electronics majoring not to mess with anything over 100 volts. That doesn't stop me from doing it, but still," he let his voice trail off, "this kind of watts? Plus, from the looks of it, there are two of them. A shield this strong would probably stop us from shooting at it. I bet if you shot a standard issue EEU at it, it wouldn't leave a mark! Nothing this strong would be allowed on the station. So whatever is in there is either very dangerous, or very deadly. Guys, I think we have just stumbled upon one of the greatest discoveries since this station was built. We have to keep this all under our hats, okay? This could be a super-computer or it could be an apocalyptic bomb. So, got any excuses why we were late?" Chris spoke very nonchalantly as though nothing had ever happened and there was no green orb. They exited the room and began walking back to the Café Probe, their original destination.

"Um, let me think. Oh yeah! Wrong turn at the elevator? Hit the wrong button?" Bob bounced ideas off him.

"Nah. Let's crawl in through the air ducts and into our usual seats. No one will miss us," Chris decided. So, they crawled through the air vents that had become a second dorm to them. At the turn, they popped up in to their designated seats. Fortunately, Jordan, who was a computer whiz, helped Chris rig up some holograms. Between the two of them, they even rigged it to perform basic functions such as yawning, sneezing, stretching, and other things. They had the chairs rigged to have trap doors under them allowing them to easily climb into their seats. Unfortunately, the air ducts were not always connected to the lunch orb. Sometimes, they would have to grab a ship and fly out there as maintenance workers. This disguise always worked. When they popped into their seats, they saw a very interesting guest speaker.

"Today is a great day for the history of exploration of the unknown! Today, we finish a ship with a 200-person seating capacity and supplies for 200 people! The fuel cells and the jet propulsion cells are in order. We have all the building completed. We have come to recruit those majoring in EEU. I would, of course, take only the students who are at the top of their classes. I will take mostly seniors, a few juniors, sophomores, and only one freshman. More of apprenticing than anything else, we are forced to take with us those majoring in Space Ship Electronics, Deep Space Design, Nuclear Chemistry, and Matter Teleportation. The setup of grades will be the same. I hope you all are interested and join us on the new journey into the unknown! This is the study-abroad program of the future!" This was an ambassador for the human exploration branch of the SETI program.

"Aren't we lucky? Those are our five majors!" Bob exclaimed happily.

"Luck might have very little to do with it. I believe that if we get on that ship, it may be all over for this station." Jordan said very quietly and suddenly. He gave everyone something to think about as they headed back to the dorms. Without realizing it, they may have become the most important people on that space station.

Once back in the dorm, watching another <u>Starship Troopers</u> on Pay-Per-View, Chris began to set the record straight. "So! Hasn't this day been quite an adventure? Let me get this straight. First, since we didn't wanna go to that assembly, we check out the glowing room. Then, we figure out that someone put a lot of work into making sure NO ONE got near that orb. As if that isn't enough, we find out that ONE freshman from each of our majors is going on a deep space mission. We take that to assume that someone else knows what we saw and feels that our time on the station needs to end. Now, if we stay on the ship, which probably will not happen, we face what we believe to be an unknown evil. If we go to the deep space odyssey, we will probably do the equivalent of dropping a nuke on this station. So, we stay here and practically write and sign our death warrants or leave and sign everyone else's. The other thing is that with the majors they have chosen, taking someone who has graduated this college in each of those, they might be planning on starting a new station. The SETI people are counting on Earth being blown up. And we are the only ones who can do anything about it! Right now, I'd rather be anyone than me! It's gonna take some work, but we will find out what we're up against! I'm going to need some things. You know the antidote to tell if someone has gone in, right? In addition, to make sure, I need 24-hour live video stream. We're gonna beat him," Chris exclaimed to the group, trying to believe himself.

They started working immediately. Rich took a break for his afternoon class while the others were hard at work. Bob was trying to figure out what exactly had a reading level that high. He could find absolutely nothing.

"I don't believe this! It's like those USAF commercials way back when: 'No one comes close.' I can't find anything! If you ask me, it's alien tech. Besides, there's no buttons or any way to work it, so I don't know what to do!"

"No one does. We are just wingin' it, so don't get mad. We're not very concerned about that at the moment. John, any luck on that powder?" Chris was taking charge again.

"Getting there, getting there," came his cool, collected response. He was mixing various elements together that created a crystal-clear powder that turned bright red 48 hours later. Hopefully, they wouldn't need it, unless whoever, or whatever came in was invisible. Chris had this prepared as a back up, hoping things never got there.

It was hard to balance their classes, homework, and trying to track down a psychopath. If the rest of the school only knew. They barely even slept. One morning, Chris fell asleep in Math class. The teacher had heard many excuses, but this was a new one.

"So, Mr. Johnson, stay up late fighting aliens again?" The class began to laugh.

It All Started In Chem Class...

Chris replied very sleepily, "You wouldn't believe me if I told you."

"I have heard everything from you!"

"Not this one, I promise," Chris replied with a gleam in his eye.

"Try me," the teacher said impatiently.

"I was trying to trap a psychopath who is going to attempt to blow up the station with a bomb," Chris said, exasperated.

"Well then go ahead! Get your sleep!" The class was stunned at his response more so than the excuse. "After all, I want to make sure you stop that psychopath! Of course, why should I worry? I have a freshman protecting my life!" At this the class began to cry. They were tears of laughter, not of fear for their lives. Chris decided to take the teacher up on this one.

"Good night! By the way, is trying to save your life a valid excuse for sleeping in class?"

"Why of course it is! Hahaha! Save my life? What a joke!" However, since Chris had read ahead in the holobook during a class the previous week, he knew all the material. Holobooks replaced textbooks, as a part of the EPA act of 2030, the year trees became a big problem. He actually went to sleep the rest of the class.

For John, however, classes were not as good. When you fall asleep in a class that deals with nuclear chemistry, you might be in a little bit of trouble. Fortunately, his task was the easiest. Soon, his bright green eyes were wide-awake and his blonde hair was combed once more. It usually took him until Wednesday to wake up, anyway. If the same could be said for the dorm, they would be in good shape. The dorm was a mess. When you work dawn till dusk, fearing for your life, you don't have time to clean.

"Guys, we need to do something about this place. It's really sad. And when a girl walks in and sees this place, she'll think I'm irresponsible and—"

"Chris, you *are* irresponsible!" John cut in. The roommates began to laugh.

"I never denied that! I just don't want to come off that way. When girls see this brown hair and my chocolate eyes, I mean *they* are *mine*, until I bring them to the dorm. That really needs to change. Let's take a well-deserved break for house-cleaning. I know you don't want to do this, but it'll help us all work faster. Then, tomorrow, we go back and set it up. What are you guys standing around for? Let's get moving here, people! What am I, the Pope? Oh, and keep in mind, pets are great at cleaning house."

They dusted the metal floor and wiped the walls. They actually did something that happened very rarely. They straightened out the sheets on their large waterbeds. They dusted the walls and put up their posters. They threw away all the empty 2-liter bottles of soda; they chucked all their dirty clothes in the washer and did several loads of laundry. It actually didn't take them very long, because they did have their pets there to help them.

"Oh man, I'm so glad we don't have homework. I'm ready to go to sleep. I will see you tomorrow!" Rich said to the others, who all shared his opinion. However, none of them slept easily.

Chapter 2: The Mission

Chris tossed and turned in his bed, not able to sleep. Of course, at 1600 hours in space, it was dark, but he began to have the feeling he was not alone. He kept dreaming of someone standing over him, ready to kill him for what he had seen. He saw someone wrapped in a cloak. The man was built much like the SETI spokesman, but was he really behind everything?

When he woke, the first thing he did was reach for his taser, which was loaded and ready under his pillow. With its illuminated sight for a flashlight, he began to walk around the dorm. A taser was a simple device to provide a nonlethal shock into people's systems, paralyzing them temporarily. When he came into the entryway and living room, he saw two other men standing there, tasers aimed at him. They were all three about to pull the trigger when someone walked in. All of them had the sights set on his forehead.

"Hey guys! You mind if I turn a light on in here? It's kinda dark," Rich said to his three roommates.

"Oh, its you!" Chris, John, and Bob all breathed a sigh of relief.

"Who were you expecting, Mr. SETI dude?" He laughed.

"That is not anywhere close to funny," Bob said.

"So, I'm guessing everyone had a few nightmares? Some cold sweats? Good, I thought it was just me. Let's check out the room. We need to get that camera set up, anyway. Jordan, you done yet?" Chris was wide awake now. He really wanted to get it taken care of, before it was too late. He got everyone a cold can of soda to help keep them awake.

"Yeah, I think it's ready. I hope it's not too big. This is as small as is possible to make. You know that, right?"

"Don't worry about it. I just hope the extreme is good enough. Got everything we need? Run the checklist!" The group bought spy equipment for such occasions as sneaking out at night.

"Grappling hook, spyglass, night-vision goggles, sword hidden in cane, light trip powder, boomerang—"

"John, why do we need a boomerang?" asked Rich irritably.

"Well, Rich, anything dangerous that needs to be activated has to be activated by the boomerang. Unless you want to try it?" Chris spoke again, with a gleam in his deep brown eyes.

"That's okay. Let's take the boomerang," Rich added, embarrassment showing in his light blue eyes. Rich, like John, had blonde hair. Rich's, however, was natural. John's was died platinum blonde, along with his goatee. Bob had died his hair also. However, he was a little more extravagant and went all-out green. His eyes were brown, but he wore red contacts. All of them thought that this was a good look for Bob. Jordan, on the other hand, had jet-black hair and hazel eyes.

"Okay, we're good! Let's move. We can't waste any more time. John, have you set the powder yet?" Chris was very alert and ready to go, the adrenaline surging through his veins.

"No. I figured we would set up the camera first. I'd rather watch it go red from the safety of my dorm than in person," John replied with a nervous laugh. They all knew that they were about to do one of the dumbest things they had ever done. However, they also realized that it might just save their lives, along with those of all the other people on that station.

"What are we standing around for? This isn't a funeral, let's go!" For once, Rich was taking charge. They moved quickly and quietly. They had no troubles until they were surprised by a noise behind them.

"Well, a good morning to you, gentlemen!" The dean of the school had just caught them out of their dorms.

"We're in so much trouble right now," Bob whispered to all the others.

"And I do hope I have found you on the way to the cafeteria to get an early start on the registration for that deep-space mission?" They were trapped. The last thing they wanted was to get on that shuttle. But at the moment, getting expelled didn't seem like the greatest idea in the world, either.

"Why of course! Unless you want us to stay here at the most influential, greatest institute of learning known to man?" Chris asked a rhetorical question. Chris and John had talked to the dean many times usually regarding extensions on their assignments. Rich took his cue and chimed in.

"We are tempted to sign up, but there is so much we would be leaving behind. We would hate to leave all the teachers we so dearly love, and talking to our best pal, our old chum—"

"Sign up for that trip or you all get *expelled!*" The dean didn't really scream, because they were in the dorm area of the station at 0230, but he still struck fear into their hearts.

"You know what? That works too! Good night, sir. Or good morning, depending on how you look at it," John added with a very nervous laugh. They then walked to the Café Probe that was always open for those nights before the exams, when you're out of coffee in the pantry. They were the first ones there. "I wonder if Dean Picklodgicer is following us," John thought aloud.

"Probably. I can't stand him! I mean, it's like us being up at this hour of the night is a cardinal sin! What is up with that? I mean, is it just me, or does it seem like every soul on this station wants to see us get on that deep-space mission? I would not be surprised to see every nerd, geek, and honor kid in the school come and say they didn't want to go on the mission, just to ensure that we did! This is weird, you know," Bob said.

"I would be more worried about getting rid of *us* than taking care of *them*," Jordan said as he waived a hand to show the rest of the college. "Perhaps, there will be various areas to sleep on the ship, organized by grade. That would make killing us easier," he said, softly, omnisciently.

Suddenly, someone walked into the probe. It was the SETI spokesman. The guys all got up and walked to the line. They spoke very casually. "So, Chris, what are you getting?" Bob tried to sound tired and not nervous. Chris yawned.

"You got any donuts?" Chris was speaking to the man behind the counter, who was deeply drinking his Mocha.

"Yeah, we got glazed, jelly-filled, chocolate-covered, custard-filled—"

"Give me a dozen powdered sugar. Don't try and tell me you're out of those, because I know you're not. Don't try and charge any more than they cost, either," Chris said, acting as though he had just awakened and didn't want to be messed with. He paid the guy and then sat down to eat, on the other end of the probe from the SETI guy. Later, his friends came and joined him. The SETI guy walked over to Chris. This made Chris very irritated and at the same time, very scared.

"Hey guys, what's up in the hood?" he said, trying to be cool.

"Who are you, why are you here, and what do you want? I'm betting the answer's no, so go away!" Chris said.

"I was the guest speaker you had yesterday. I have talked to your teachers, and they tell me you are the top of the grade in each major!"

"I told you, the answer's no! Our teachers hate us, we're the biggest slackers in school, and on top of that, the dean himself nearly expelled us! The dean! So don't go trying to tell me we're the cream of the freshmen crop, 'cause that's bull! I'm sorry, did you want something?"

"Listen, I know skill when I see it! We want you on that shuttle! The SETI program wants you on that shuttle," he exuberantly yelled, playing the part very well.

"Okay, now I'm interested. Who, exactly, told you that we were cut out for the shuttle mission?" Bob was talking, since Chris had already shown his disinterest in the subject.

"I am on strict orders not to say," he replied worriedly. Chris thought he could see the beads of sweat beginning to roll down his forhead as he glanced around the room.

"What are you guys afraid of? What kind of harm could we cause to the almighty SETI program? Is your boss afraid that we're gonna track his home down and nuke it? Give me a break!

It All Started In Chem Class... 15

What could a bunch of college kids do to you anyway? And why is it so important that we go on that mission? Is there something you know about that we don't? I can't take this! I'm outta here! Are you guys coming or staying here and listening to this idiot babble on about us being the best kids in the school?"

"Chris, dude, cool down! It's okay." John was surprised. Chris never blew up like this in public.

"Sorry, his girlfriend broke up with him yesterday; he still hasn't gotten over her," Rich lied quickly. "What he meant to say was that we need some time to think it over. We're not exactly morning people, so we need some more time to think about it. We need to talk to our teachers and find out what we would miss and stuff like that. No offense to the SETI program, but this isn't as simple as blinking an eye. So, can we get back to you on it?"

"Well, let's just hope the other slots don't fill up," he said, putting emphasis on the last words.

"Yeah, let's hope not," John said.

"Well, then I'll be on my way."

"He's wired," Rich told the group. "While you had class, I made up another wire, with an even smaller monitor. Let's take a look," he said as he pulled out the monitor. When they looked at it, they were stunned. They saw a man dressed with a hat covering his face enter the room and close the door behind him. He walked up to the generator and put a small key card or some type of card into it. Suddenly, a vast array of lights appeared on the far side of the room. He walked over and summoned up a picture of a person. Of all people, it was the dean of the school.

"I think they know more than they're letting on, sir," he said in a whisper.

"These walls are soundproof, I had them built myself. Now, about the freshmen," he said evilly.

"They know more than they should, even though they won't let on. I think we can handle it," he said with a small laugh. Then, before they heard anymore, the feed cut off.

"He took off the bug. On or off that ship, we have so much trouble. We can go down there and confront him, or we can sit around and stay out of trouble for once in our lives. All up for staying out of trouble?" Chris knew this was a rhetorical question. None of them liked staying out of trouble. They all lived life on the edge. "All up for not confronting them?" All the hands were in the air. "Let's get some sleep, Okay? Well, the mission failed, but oh well." They all dispersed quietly, as though nothing had happened that fateful morning.

They woke up a few hours later in much higher spirits than they were in when sleep took them. They ate breakfast, drank some soda, and went to class, because it was a Thursday. All students had a full-day class on Thursday so no one stayed in the dorm, which was good. They all dreaded the thought of being alone, fearing for their lives. Classes went well, and Chris had a very interesting time is his class. Some guy Chris knew was throwing pencils into the ceiling. Chris was watching and laughing at him. He figured that would get him in trouble. However, it kept his mind off of whatever evil scheme was being hatched against him. It also took his mind off of his schoolwork. "So, Chris, as I was saying, if I wanted to create 400 watts of power, how many amps would I need?" the teacher asked him, knowing he would not know.

"Uhh, it depends on your voltage. You need the amps multiplied by the volts to equal the wattage, so if you did it correctly, I would recommend using a 50-volt system with 80 amps, or you can use other things— that would just be the most efficient."

"Well, Mr. Johnson, the answer was 'You can't find out without knowing the voltage,' but I will accept your response as well. You will have a test over this material tomorrow. I hope you are prepared, and I will see you again, hopefully not until our next class. Until then, so long!" Everyone began exiting their class, ready to go back to the dorms.

"We've got to go back! We have to know what's going on," John told everyone.

"And risk getting caught or expelled? We can't!" Rich argued.

"They know we're on to them, so our time is borrowed. What can we do? If you ask me, before we do anything, we need a high-level SETI security card. That thing unleashed all the secrets in the room. Unless the dean and that SETI dude wind up dead, we have to get on the space mission. Not for our sake, I'm saying they won't allow us to do otherwise." Chris was all-of-a-sudden very worked up about the whole situation. "Everyone going to the Spaceball game tonight?"

"We're *playing* tonight. We're all on the team right? You can be such a *blonde* sometimes! Wake up, Chris!" John said. Spaceball didn't have positions, just a team of five.

"Oh no! We missed practice. I completely forgot about it! Let's see if the coach is mad. By the way, I had the flu, right?" Chris said.

"If I had bronchitis, then Rich had it too. When a roommate gets sick, all the roommates get sick is the way I see it. Bronchitis is very contagious, you know!" Bob answered cheerfully.

"Let's just all get bronchitis. It takes a week to heal anyway," Chris said as an afterthought. So, they walked—trotted rather—to Coach Beale's office. He was in his office, sitting comfortably with his feet on his desk. He didn't look up until Bob broke the silence. They were all very anxious, because missing practice was horrible.

CHAPTER 3: THE SPACEBALL GAMES

Chris explained their predicament, and fortunately, Coach Beale understood the situation. Soon, they were back to being the league favorite (they made up an entire team, with no back-ups). They knew that Spaceball was the biggest, as well as only sport in space.

Spaceball is a combination of a lot of sports, all rolled into one. Everyone played on Spaceboards. They played in space, which gave them the ability to hover/fly. There was no set offense or defense. In that respect, it was similar to basketball. There were five people; offense meant they had the ball, and defense meant they did not. The same people played regardless. No equipment had to be changed, either, which led to the fluidity of the sport.

Players could kick, throw, fly, hit, or pitch the ball. The interesting thing about the Spaceball itself was that it was similar to a sponge in that it had the ability to change sizes. It was self-propelled and programmed to move of its own accord. Chris was the captain. There were no positions. This was one reason that Spaceball was different from everything else in the world of sports. Chris decided what each person was supposed to do, based on the type of move they were doing. Sometimes everyone would block for one person. It didn't matter as long as they got it in the Abyss. The Abyss was the most dangerous area of the playing field. It had a blinding light that was used to distract players, as well as a laser beam trip that would activate a barrier of fire around the Abyss, and an electromagnet that would mess up the polarity of the board. Thanks to all the money Chris's dad made as an eye surgeon, Chris had one of the best boards. He also had a top quality baton, which each player was allowed to have. They were allowed to have special polyeurocarbonate armor, which was small, light, and very strong.

Chris had a pet tiger that also played with him. Pets that had the special suit, and some mode of transportation, were

It All Started In Chem Class...

allowed. His tiger moved with jetpacks, not a Spaceboard. He even had the suit designed to give his tiger longer, stronger arms with opposable thumbs. After much training, the tiger got used to it. He was one of the best feline players.

The games were between Fraternities. Chris, Bob, Jordan, John, and Rich made up one of the teams, the D^3 team. They were a good team, maybe even the best. This game, however, they were playing the dreaded Alpha Alpha Alpha team, the best in the league except for the Trip D's, as they were known in slang terms. The entire college was showing up for this game, regardless of whether or not they even followed Spaceball. If they won their third game, they would be undefeated. In the first two games, the beat the two worst teams in the division. So far, it had been a cakewalk for the D^3s. This would be their first real challenger.

"Okay! This had better be a good fight, er, game that is, because there is a lot more stuff I should be doing right now. I want a clean game. Now for the coin toss. Trip A's, call it in the air!" the ref said to get the game going. This was, of course, the only part of the game that took place inside the stands, because if you toss a coin in open space, which means actual space, where there is zero gravity, you have to bring it back down.

"Tails," the captain, who was among the best players on the campus, said. The coin showed a picture of a Spaceball. This was heads in the game, which used a specially designed quarter.

"Delta-3, you gonna take it out or give it away?" Delta-3 was the freshmen team's nickname, because it was easier than saying "D to the third." These were the winner's options. Most people, almost all Spaceball players, would take the ball, giving them the first, and if successful, only shot at scoring. In Spaceball, the team to gain the most points, determined by the number of times the Spaceball was cast into the Abyss would win. The team members of D-3 were not most people.

"What else would we do with it? We'll give it away. Make life interesting," Chris chuckled.

"Which way you want to face?" In Spaceball, you stayed in facing one direction the entire game.

"Away from the sun, as tradition should hold," Chris said.

"*Let the games begin!* Gentlemen, start your engines," the only ref said. He then threw the ball to the Delta-Threes.

"Boys, ya wanna make it interesting?" Chris first squeezed the ball, making it shrink, cast it backwards, to John, who then returned it. They began to throw the ball around so fast no one could see where it was. Then Rich, who was in the back of their setup, spun around at lightning speed and chucked it high, far, and fast. Since the Spaceball is white, it cannot be seen against the sun. It hit the other team's captain right in the forehead. He was stunned; he couldn't even reach the ball. However, one of his teammates grabbed it and sped off toward the Abyss.

In Spaceball, fouls were nonexistent, because if it even remotely *looked* like an accident, the ref wouldn't call it. Chris's team, like so many others, had already planned many "accidents."

Chris called to John and Rich, who were already set up: "Give this gentleman a reason to cry!" They did, too. They slammed into him at full speed, like an oncoming train. John saw another man coming, and swerved out of the way, just as Rich swooped down to avoid the swing of an opposing baton, because clubbing was encouraged in Spaceball. The three all met, but John and Rich had two hands on their batons. Of course, it did not penetrate his grass-green armor, although it did throw him off balance and cause him to do a somersault, which received boisterous applause from the audience. The guy from the Trip-A's prided himself on riding unstrapped, which simply meant he didn't strap his feet in. Upon flipping, he grabbed his board, dropping the Spaceball.

The Spaceball, which was designed to do the job of the refs in hitting all who made wrong moves, slammed into Rich's stomach, which was part of the plan. This gave John the perfect opportunity to grab the Spaceball. The announcer was going crazy.

"And the Trip-A goes speeding off, protected by two men. It looks like John 'The J-turn' Smith is going for a cutoff, alongside Rich 'Cashed-Out' Flithinteon, but *no*, they swerve out

It All Started In Chem Class…

at the last men, and SLAM right into the man with the ball, a Mr. Sean Rackombosajoyo, causing him to flip over and *lose the Spaceball!*

"What? It has once again taken on a mind of its own, flying straight into Cashed-Out's stomach! John, making a famous J-Turn from beside Rich, grabs the Spaceball. This is, of course, putting it into the Triple-Delta possession for the first time in this game!

"This is crucial, as the game is an hour long. In the event that no one has scored after that time, it will immediately become a sudden death. That means, for those of you who aren't avid Spaceball watchers, that the game will either last one hour, or until the first score, assuming that it takes longer than one hour. Getting possession now means they might have the first chance to— never mind!

"The ball has been passed to Chris, who is going very high up into the arena space. He appears to be going for Stunt Points, which is determined by how risky the executions of scoring runs are. Suddenly Alex Gomanahezera is chasing him, attempting to make a steal for high Stunts. They are going to the top of the space arena, Chris easily passing him by, and reaching the top of the dome. He rides along the top, waiting for Alex to get up. Perhaps Alex is just going for the ball, because following someone else scores next to no Stunt Points."

"It should be noted that while Stunt Points have no real value, they *do* show how risky the plays are in the game. Alex attempts to chase him, knowing it's useless. Chris checks down, sees the others setting up. He is making a vertical U-turn, and heading back for his own Abyss!"

Chris took care of this problem with Alex. He swerved, left, right, dipped down, then shot up, flipping upside down while waving the Spaceball. He did a complete mid-air, inverted, $180°$ turn around in the blink of an eye. He sped off down the arena, but the Triple-Alpha team made a habit of leaving two of their men to guard their own Abyss, while the other three chased him, one on each side and one behind, setting up for the 5-Sided Dice Run. This move, made famous by the Alpha Alpha Alpha, was where all five players would gather around one person from the other team, boxing him in like five of the six sides of a dice, leaving his only option in the Abyss. One of them would then trigger the firewall, leaving him to burn. Chris was expecting this but wasn't prepared for how quickly they could execute it. Before he knew it, they had already set up, although they were still four meters from the Abyss. Chris's tiger, Comet flew up behind the Tri-A man, who was directly behind Chris, and using his genetically-enhanced intelligence, hit him on the head. He then flew straight into his board, causing it to flip. This gave Chris an opportunity to escape, which he took. He flew straight to the ground, flipped up and sped toward his own goal, and the audience began to cheer. The audience loved Comet, who was named for his orange fur and fiery jetpack.

"*Incredible!* I've never seen the Triple-Alpha team's infamous dice roll escaped! Chris Johnson is truly incredible! Yet again, he is speeding towards his own goal, but wait, what's this? He is riding the bottom side of the arena, back towards the Tri-A goal, almost daring them to attempt the dice run again. He does seem insane, but it always works for him. He appears to be meeting his tiger at Midpoint, the Spaceball equivalent of half-court or the 50-yard line. The tiger landed on his shoulder, and takes a hold on the Spaceball. I bet they didn't expect this!

"And the tiger is off, living up to his name, looking like nothing more than a comet, or a blur, for that matter. The freshmen Delta-Delta-Delta team, commonly referred to as Team D^3 is going for the next-to-impossible feat of the pet score, which gains a vast number of Stunt Points, if it is properly executed. *Yes*, they are going to do it! The five pets, Chris's tiger in the lead, followed on the right by Rich's husky and John's cobra and on the left and Jordan's monkey and Bob's peregrine falcon on the right.

It All Started In Chem Class... 23

For those of you who don't know, Bob is a new student from Alaska. Here they come, while their owners remain at their Abyss to watch, all hope entrusted to Comet, Bigpaw, Sting, Eddy, and Fenix!

"The only way to counter such a move, one which is even more difficult, is to use the pets of your own team. Off go the Triple-Alpha team animals, which include a lion, a grizzly bear, a wolf, a gorilla, and a crow. On Team Triple-Alpha, they value size more than they value other qualities. This could prove to decide the entire match, because Team D^3 has relatively small animals compared to the beasts of Team Triple-Alpha. And here they come, attempting to head off Comet! But Comet dodges left, ducks down, flies up, and—what's this? It appears as though Bob's falcon, Fenix, is performing his famous swooping attack in a last attempt to protect Comet. He runs head-on into the Tri-A grizzly, known as Crusher. This slightly delays their attack, as Comet races across the field towards the Alpha Abyss. However, Crusher is only dazed after such an impact, and soon returns! They are flying, all at their fastest, going, going, going to the Abyss. Who will win? I'm on the edge of my seat; I can't take the suspense!"

John felt the same way. He couldn't do anything except watch. His cobra, Sting, was easily the smallest animal in the court, so it was very fragile, even with its armor. But, he was also the most agile. Sting had his ups and downs, but he was very good at distracting other animals. He knew that crows, such as the opponent's pet Blackbeak, and snakes tended to be predator and prey. This played well to their advantage. Blackbeak was watching Sting, not only because of their natural born hate for each other, but because that was how he was trained. Through genetic engineering, the animals understood much more than their ancestors could have. They were almost as smart as Homo sapiens. Almost. As they neared the Abyss, John's tension was growing. He knew what they might try. All the athletes could communicate with their animals with special intercom systems installed in the suits. He had to get Sting ready. He spoke into his suit, "Sting, they're gonna give it to you. Get ready."

Chris knew what he had to do. He said into his spacesuit, "Give it to Sting, then hit Blackbeak, you know, the bird, as hard as you can. Make it look like a faulty jet pack." Comet was familiar with all these terms, through many hard months of training. Then Chris said to the rest of the team, "Set up a defense for Cobra and Comet. They're the only two that matter at this point."

Jordan tensed. His monkey would take the brunt of an attack from Wolfenstein, the large white wolf of the other team. His only chance was to outmaneuver the wolf, which would be difficult. Even with the special armor, getting smashed by a wolf can hurt a lot.

"They are right at the Abyss, with no sign of anyone slowing down! It seems like the Triple-A animal fleet is preparing an attack, er, accident rather. They set it up, and as they do, Bob's Falcon, Jordan's monkey, and Rich's husky line up to take the attack. Comet swings out, up, down, and slows down. Comet seems to be having jetpack trouble; apparently one engine is defective. He loses control of the Spaceball, right as the Tri-A team attacks! Their wolf, Wolfenstein, brutally hits Eddy, the monkey! Excuse me, I am mistaken! Eddy ducked, singing Wolfenstein's armor with his jets! What a maneuver! As Comet releases the Spaceball, due to his defective jet, he *slams* right into Blackbeak, the other team's crow! Oh, that was *brutal!* The cobra, Sting, coils up, protected by the rest of his team, and suddenly, using his chain of rockets, uncoils in what can only be a throw of the Spaceball, right into the *abyss!* Eddy, who took off immediately after dodging Wolfenstein, sets up right above the point where the Spaceball will land. Eddy hits it with his tail,

It All Started In Chem Class…

sending it downward! Within the last three meters of the Abyss, as most of you should know, the Spaceball directs its jets in a straight down angle, scoring the win! I don't *believe it!*

"Wow, what a game! Talk about a crowd pleaser; that was *incredible!*

T"he Delta Delta Delta team never ceases to amaze us. And yet, both teams advance to the semi-finals, because this season is a double-elimination, which means that if two teams with perfect records meet in the semis, they both face another semi-finalist, and so on and so forth until only two teams remain! Thanks folks, have a great weekend. This is Patrick Noble, saying good night. Good night!"

CHAPTER 4: THE LIST

The players went back to their dorms, bringing their animals with them. They all slept like the dead that night. The win had put all thoughts of aliens, SETI, and space trips out of sight and out of mind. The next day, though, all of that came back to them. "Hey guys, they posted who's goin' on the deep-space mission," Rich said to the room filled with his friends.

"Ooh, the suspense is killing me; let's go see who the lucky people are!" John said with an obvious tone of sarcasm in his voice. But still, they went to see the posters. They were shocked at what they saw. It was not at all what they expected.

"*What?* We didn't make it? But, that's not right. We were supposed to make it . . . Everyone knew we would. I mean, even the dean said we would. It just doesn't add up," Chris said.

"Hello, gentlemen," the dean said. "Find anything that—I don't know—surprises you?" He had seen the results, obviously.

"No sir, not a thing. Just looking to see who gets shipped off, er, rather, goes on the fun, interesting, exciting trip," Bob replied with a grin.

"Really. Are you on the list?"

"No sir!"

"Hmm, that's surprising, isn't it?" the dean retorted with a smirk.

"Not to me, sir; I never expected to make it. I mean, come on, I'm a slacker. Point blank. Slacker. That's all there is to it. Did *you* think I could do it?" Chris answered with the best look of sincerity he could muster.

"I sent the dean's list to them. All of you are on my list. Believe me, you *are* on my list."

"The dean . . . the dean attempting comedy? I don't believe it!" John couldn't help himself, stifling a laugh.

"I'm not joking. I sent in your names, and they weren't taken. Do you have any idea why?"

"Not a clue, honestly," Chris said.

It All Started In Chem Class...

"Nope, not me," Rich chimed in.

"Huh? Whoa, why are you looking at me? I don't know anything about the...well, never mind." Bob answered, taking his appointed role as the guilty party.

"My thinking was that you went against what I told you and didn't sign up!" The dean thrust forth an accusing finger at Chris, who backed up.

"Ask the guy in the Café Probe—he saw us put them in there," Chris said.

"Really? Then I will ask him."

"Dean, ya wanna know what *I* think? I think you took them out of the box, just to have a reason to expel me. That's what I think."

"I think I can expel you just for that!"

"Why sir, I never thought I'd hear expel associated with *my* name," Chris exclaimed in utter shock and disbelief, lunging backwards as his brown eyes grew with feigned astonishment..

"So, what ever happened to those applications?"

"I believe we told you, sir; we sent them in," John replied, with a much more serious tone to his voice.

"Well, I'll try and pull some strings, to ensure you get on there," Dean Roberts said. He continued, "I know how much you want to go."

"Oh yeah," Chris said, half-heartedly, "can't wait."

"Have a good class gentlemen." And with that, he walked off.

"He is so *annoying!* I can't stand that guy!" John was obviously angry about his "pulling strings" as the Dean had called it.

"What is so important about that trip, anyway? It doesn't make sense," Chris stated with frustration.

"I think SETI knows something we don't," Bob said.

"Ah, who cares? I think we need to figure out who transferred those forms from the place where we put them in to the place they didn't turn up. Now, who would know who that is?" Rich wondered aloud.

"SETI man!" Bob seemed happy, oddly enough. So, they went off to find the SETI agent. On the way there, they passed the Triple-Alpha frat club.

"Hey, nice game! I never thought you'd pull off that ending. Man, that was a great show of tactics. We'll get ya in the finals!" The captain of the team yelled from inside the room.

"Assuming, of course, that we even *see* you in the finals," Chris laughed. We just kept walking. Then a thought dawned on Chris.

"Hey, did you guys see that SETI lecturer person at the game yesterday?"

One of the other players said, "Yeah, I did; he was sitting with the Alpha-Delta guys. Ya need anything else?"

"Well, you heard they wanna do a tag-team tournament?" Jordan asked.

"Yep, I heard about that! What, you wanna team up?"

"Sure!"

"Okay, let's do that then. See you guys later."

"Bye." Then we went down to the Alpha-Delta frat club, and sure enough, we found the SETI spokesman. "Hello, sir!"

"Yes, can I help you with something?" He sounded impatient.

"Yes, you can. Who delivered those forms from the Café Probe?"

"Actually, it was Billy from this fraternity."

"Billy, we need a word with you," I said to the kid he had indicated. Fortunately, we all still had on our armor and batons on us. The armor was flexible, so we just rolled it under our sleeves, and the batons were retractable. "We put our forms in there, but they weren't received. Do you have any idea what happened?" They had all stepped out of the room, and out of earshot from the people inside.

"Yeah, I do. I took them out of the boxes. I took out all the Spaceball players."

"Why?"

It All Started In Chem Class...

"I heard they planned to use us as just the dumb jocks, their guinea pigs. They would send us out first, sort of the "take them, we'll live without" strategy. I didn't want any of us to have to do that. Make sense?"

Chris spoke up. "Yeah, that makes plenty of sense. Billy, of all the freshmen, they would have picked us. You did us a big favor when you did that. Thanks, man. What did you do with the forms?"

"Burned them with a chemical acid that leaves no trace," he replied with a grin.

"Good work! Bye Billy," Chris said. With those words of closing, they left. "So, Rich, you think Dean Picklodgicer will get us on that accursed ship after all?"

"I bet he'll use the excuse of 'We want the whole universe exposed to the great sport of Spaceball and the greatest team the sport will ever know!'"

"Yeah, you're probably right. I just don't know how we can avoid it! Man, I wish I knew what SETI is planning," Bob said. They walked, sort of accidentally, to the Dean's office. Bob knocked. "Telegram for a Ms. De-Ann Pickloadedjicker. Is this where we might find Ms. Pickloadedjicker?"

"There is no one here . . . Oh, it's you five again. How may I help you?"

"Dean Picklodgicer, were you ever involved in the SETI program?" Rich asked curiously.

"As a matter of fact, I was. I still am. And why might you ask? Do you know something I don't know you know? About me?"

"Of course we don't! Why Dean, why would you *ever* suspect us of such trickery?" Jordan asked dubiously

"You know I have my reasons! Now tell me, why would you suspect my relations with the SETI program?" The Dean was really mad at them now.

"We saw the spokesperson from SETI sitting with the Alpha-Delta fraternity, and isn't that your former fraternity?"

"Yes, as a matter of fact, I am an alumnus from the Alpha-Delta, a charter member, you could go so far as to say, a founder of it. Anything else?"

Jordan answered, "Nope, that's it." They walked on in silence, each developing his own theory about it. Jordan's mind was reeling. *The guy from SETI communicated to the Dean via a secret panel in a secret room; he sat with the Dean's former frat group. The dude from the frat group saved our butts. So what is the common thread?* He wondered.

John pieced together the puzzle in his own way. *It's the frat group*, he thought to himself, *it's gotta be the frat group! But then Billy, what was that about? A setup maybe? I don't get why they'd do that. Those guys are both total weirdoes.*

Chris wasn't sure what to believe. *If the Dean was part of SETI, he knew the spokesman before he worked here. So, whatever they're doing was set up a while ago. But why are we so important?*

Is it really about Spaceball? Could it be that simple? Rich wondered. *I mean, we are the best of friends, but is that the common thread? Wait! That's it!*

"Jordan, approximately how long has the sport of Spaceball existed?" Jordan was the expert on Spaceball and its history.

"about 30 or 40 years. Why?"

"That's it! The common thread!"

Chris wondered aloud, "Wha?"

Rich replied, "It's what connects us, the dean, and the SETI guy. Bob, run me that guy's career. His name is Max. Max Groveland."

"Okay, I think I see where you're going with this," Bob said as he did what was requested of him. "So, you were right. Listen to this: 'Max Groveland was a part of the team that won the first International Spaceball Tournament, along with Joe Picklodgicer, who is now Dean of the International Space Station and University. The game was played 25 years ago this coming April.'" Spaceball had been tried before the ISSU, but had not become popular until the fraternities started playing. That was why it was not widely known that the dean and the SETI agent had played on the same team.

Chris's mind was racing. "April, April, April," he muttered aloud. "What's in April? Hmm. Wait, that's it! That's when they plan to do the mission. Starting date is April 24th. What day was it played?"

"April 25th," Bob answered dubiously, looking cockeyed at Jordan.

"So they leave the day before the anniversary of their first Spaceball game. All of this is related to Spaceball, huh? Weird," Chris said, shaking his head.

Bob stared at Chris. "Man, you're insane! This has *nothing* to do with Spaceball! That's obviously just where they met. This is *way* deeper than Spaceball. I bet that's just a cover-up for something else. Trust me, SETI is like CIA, just in space. The dean is pretty crazy too. Besides, what would a deep-space mission or a supercomputer or a conspiracy theory have to do with Spaceball?"

Rich spoke up and said, "I want one more look at that green orb."

Chris yawned. "How about we just go to sleep? And by the way, what day is it?"

John answered, "Sunday." With that, they all wandered back to their own section of the dorm to sleep.

CHAPTER 6: THE SENIOR FINALS

"Hey, you going to the game Friday?" John asked them all the next morning.

"The Senior Spaceball Champs? Yeah," Chris replied. The Spaceball tournament existed in four separate stages, according to grade. Each grade of the frat had a different abbreviation. The senior group of Delta-Delta-Delta was abbreviated Team 3D. However, they were not as good as their freshmen class, and were currently in last place, one loss from totalus, the "official" term for elimination. They would be competing on Thursday, to attempt to place in the finals. The other Delta-Delta-Delta teams were required to go. The Friday match was only required if 3D placed, which they probably would not do. "Thursday's match is gonna be boring," Chris commented.

"At least it'll be quick and painless," Jordan sighed, "Those poor souls don't have a chance! I mean, even *we're* better than them."

"That's it! Jordan, you're a genius!" Chris exclaimed.

"Huh? I mean, duh, I knew that!"

"Sure ya did. Anyway, would it be truly illegal and immoral to switch out a couple of our players with a couple of theirs?" Chris asked.

"Yes, it would. I'm sure you want to try it?"

"Sometimes, I think you guys know me too well," Chris replied. "So, who should we throw in there?"

"Uh, Chris, shouldn't we check with them, first?" John said.

"Great idea! They're just down this hall right here," Chris said. They turned left thinking that the 3D room was there. "Uh, I thought it was, anyway. . . This is odd, I don't see it. I must have taken a wrong turn back there!"

"Thanks a lot, Chris, you just got us lost!" Rich exclaimed. They found their way back to the 3D room. They found the room empty, save the team.

It All Started In Chem Class...

"Hey guys. How was practice?" The captain seemed uninterested, but making conversation none the less.

Jordan was the first to respond. "That coach is a slave driver. He made us do a twin double-helix with active space mines! Have you guys started yet?"

"We leave later tonight. He's gonna work us hard, too," Jim, who was the captain, said. "But it's Okay, because by Thursday, team AGN won't stand a chance! Those silly Greeks think they can beat us! Ha!" AGN stood for Alpha-Gamma-Nu; they came up with the name due to the fact that its founding members were Greek. It was intended to be a pun: AGN and Aegean.

Another team member, Bill, chimed in, saying, "Yeah, we got Keno here from India, and this boy can fly like you ain't never seen before! He's gonna blow them away!" And with that, they left for practice.

"So, Chris, still planning to pull the old switch-a-roo?" John asked, grinning. Chris shrugged.

"Nope, I'll see how their new Indian guy does. Should be a good match." After three more days of intense practicing, and boring classes, the Senior Semi-Finals were at last taking place. Chris and the rest of the team took their usual seats, on the 3D side. The game started with 3D receiving the Spaceball, and passing it right to Keno. They set up a defensive maneuver, called a 4-man star run. This maneuver gets its name from the fact that the players form a star, or a cross, and rotate around the central person, warding off attacks with their batons. They then spun in a new direction, circling forwards and backwards. By alternating the star run and the spinning cross, the other team was in complete bewilderment, as was the announcer.

"Folks, welcome to the last chance for these two teams, Team AGN and Team 3D. This is within the first minute of play, and Team 3D is performing incredibly difficult tactics already! They are switching between two maneuvers, commonly known as the star run and the spinning cross. The other team has no idea what to do! They move as one, a single unit. They are going towards the roof, leveling out in a lateral star run, and resume motion! I don't believe this! I've never seen such difficult tactics put into use by this, one of the two worst teams in the league! I think this might simply be warming up for the Finals, tomorrow night, which they seem fairly set on going to!

"They are already at the Abyss! Their newest member, Keno Stupehsmall, is a superb flyer! His Spaceboard technique is unchallenged by this league! He has diverted all sorts of attempts to shlack him. Shlacking, for those of you who are new to the sport, is the art of taking away the Spaceball. Some people are getting through the star trick, but not many. They seem to be hovering around the Abyss."

Keno was ready. It was his big move, the one thing that could permanently make or break his Spaceball career. He had to dive straight through the lateral star, which was about to take out the other team entirely. His job was simple. Hit at an angle, trigger the firewall to give him rear defense, and slam the Spaceball right smack into the Abyss. He noticed the slightest bit of slowing down by his own team. That was his sign. He had practiced this every day for the last two weeks. This was his biggest shot, except for the only other move he could do. That, however, he would have to save for Friday night.

"What's this? I think I just saw a slight waiver in the star motion! Could this be setting something up? Both teams are tense. I think Keno might be attempting something. What, I don't have any idea. Yes, this must be indicative of some great finishing move! I can feel the crowd's tension. They have gone dead silent, waiting for something, anything, to happen! And off goes Keno, racing straight through the star formation. That is risky flying on his part. What's this? The formation broke just in time! They have apparently spun out in a spiral, knocking Team AGN right off their boards, which were unstrapped, do to the long time of inaction by Team 3D. Wow, what a great show of strategy! And it appears as though Keno, still relatively new to the sport, accidentally tripped the firewall! That's not good," the announcer said, not realizing the intent of this mistake. He continued, "The

It All Started In Chem Class...

other team, all of whom are from Greece, are getting back onto their boards, shaken, but not bruised, due to the armor. They attempt to chase after Keno, who has not yet deposited the Spaceball."

Keno had just done it. The wall was up, he hit the polarity adjustment switch, and killed his board's power. He waited, watching the watch on his wrist tick away. One minute left. If he shot now, he would still give Team AGN a chance at winning. He couldn't do that. Thirtyseconds left. Beads of sweat began to appear. He was nervous. Most of the school was there. It was being shown across the globe on international television. He knew his family was at home, watching his every move. The watch counted down. Ten, nine, eight, seven, six. Suddenly, the biggest person on Team AGN, known simply as Slugger, was flying down at him. He had to drop it! But, in this instance, the Spaceball was a wild card. It was highly likely that it could fly right into Slugger's grasp. Even with the armor, Slugger would pound his head in with his baton. He turned his board back on, Slugger just millimeters away. His little wristwatch said the match would end officially in five seconds. He hadn't planned on someone bypassing the firewall. *This is it,* he thought, *it's over. I'm over. One quick hit and it'll all be over.* But it wasn't! He suddenly found himself, without even thinking about it, spiraling down, swinging from side wall to side wall. Three seconds left, and Slugger was still at the same height he had been. He had been making absolutely no motion. His board was stalled! Keno took out his baton, a grin forming on his face, and before he could stop himself, he slammed it into Slugger's board! With Slugger completely unaware, he simply dropped the Spaceball. It flew back up, and he hit it once more, scoring just as the buzzer for the end of the regulation time sounded.

"Keno Stupehsmall has just advanced his teams to the big games Friday night! Tomorrow night will be the final semi-final and then the finals! It should be quite an incredible show! Once again, ladies and gentlemen, this is Patrick Noble saying good morning, good afternoon, good evening and good night, whichever time zone you are in!"

"Woohoo! Go Keno! Good job, my man! Now get back to your room and get some sleep! We got a big game tomorrow. Two of them, actually," Jim said. They left, all very excited, and also very tired.

Classes seemed a blur the next day for everyone. A Spaceball double-header final would draw the entire world. Team 3D had practice three times that day, excused from classes. They had a lot to go over, a lot of routines to practice. One such routine was appropriately named the "Suicidal Slapstick." This move was so named for the fact that it much resembled something right out of a Stooges film. It made them look stupid, and the tactic seemed all-out pointless. The purpose of the tactic was quite similar to the purpose of the three stooges. It was to make people laugh. The suicidal portion of its nickname was due to the fact that they attacked each other with their batons. This was most often used when other teams came to watch your training. It was rarely used in an actual match, unless it was a guaranteed loss. Chris and his team went to the practice, in part to give their elders advice. Chris was amazed at what he saw.

"The suicidal slapstick? Why would you ever think to use that in the *semi-finals?*" Chris yelled through his microphone.

"Trust me man, just watch," Jim said. They lined up into a vertical V formation. Then the top two turned on reverse engines, causing them to fall down. They brought out their batons and clotheslined the people beside them. They then flipped around and hit the bottom man, causing pandemonium. They all began flying back and forth, hitting each other. However, there was the slowest progression towards the Abyss that if you weren't watching closely, you would not notice. Team Delta-Delta-Delta figured out the strategy. As they continued to brutally beat each other, the team went right above the Abyss. Then, in what appeared to be a shot to the head, Jim instead hit the Spaceball right into the Abyss, scoring, and what would have been winning if it had been an actual competition.

It All Started In Chem Class...

"Wow," Chris said, "I'm impressed."

"Thanks," Jim replied dryly. "I just wish that meant practice was over. Sadly, we've got one more thing to go over."

"Cool! What is it?" Rich asked.

"It's a little something we call the five-man free-for-all. Basic idea is that we form a rectangle, with one man in the middle. Then we set up around the Abyss, with the same central man. We begin to hit the Spaceball to the middle man, and he hits it to someone else. Then—the same as in that old game Pong—it gets faster and faster and faster. The whole time, we fend off the other team."

Chris asked, "What if they get all of you and the middle man covered?"

"Actually, the move more resembles pinball. We are all spinning, just barely aware of who has the Spaceball. We talk through the microphones, and that's how we know when to be ready. The spinning bit of it protects us from attacks. The middle man is stationary. You wanna see it?"

John answered, "Sure." They took off, setting up at the Abyss immediately, and began to spin. They hit the ball back and forth until it reached fast speeds. It became nothing more than a blur. Suddenly, the captain, Jim, hit it to Keno, the middle man, and Keno hit it straight down. It was a sure-fire move. Chris flipped through the holoplaybook. Holobooks were the books of the future. They were small, round machines that would project an image into mid-air, called a hologram. These holograms would resemble the written pages which were their predecessors. They were smaller, had larger print, and were easier to read. They had eight plays ready, and only two games, at most, left to play. This gave them a wide variety of options. But, their practice was over, and Team Alpha-Beta-Gamma, a.k.a. Team 123, was practicing next. They were set to be in the finals, and had an incredible team. It would take more than a show of comedy to beat them. But, Team 3D had to first beat Team Delta-Omega-Gamma, Team DOG. The two teams went back to their dormitories, and waited.

"Welcome everyone to the much anticipated Senior Spaceball Finals double-header. The crowd here is ready to go; it's a sold-out game! Tonight we have two teams competing for a shot in the finals, but only one can go. We have one team eagerly awaiting the finals; they are already one of the finalists as a result of last Wednesday's win. So first, please welcome the first team to be in the finals, *Team Alpha-Beta-Gamma!*" The crowd roared as they flew out onto the field and occupied five chairs marked "Reserved for Finalists." They were dressed in their usual red costumes, each branded on the sleeve with the words "Spaceball Championship."

The announcer resumed. "Now, please welcome, for the first game of our double-header, *Team Delta Omega Gamma!*" All the supporters of the team screamed and shouted as they flew on to the field, and took their seats. "Team Delta-Omega-Gamma is made up of members from China, Korea, and Japan. But, this is only one of our two teams, so now, please turn your attention to the other end of the field, where we are now joined by Team *Delta-Delta-Delta!*" Everyone on the other three Delta teams screamed and shouted, while secretly uttering stuff into their microphones. There weren't as many supporters of Team 3D, mainly because they advanced to the semi-finals by a couple of lucky shots. "Team 3D is joined by Keno Stupehsmall, their newest member from India, who has already earned the nickname the 'Asian bullet.' This should be quite a game. The team captains are on now in the stands for the coin toss. Let's listen in," Patrick said.

"Alright, I want a good, clean fight from both of you. Team DOG, you call it in the air," the referee said.

"Tails," the captain, known as Hwango, said.

"Tails it is. You gonna keep it or give it?"

"We will take it," he replied.

"Great words by a great man. That is Hwango. His name in Chinese is really long, so he just prefers Hwango. Team DOG is gonna take the Spaceball. They will have the first possession. So Team 3D has to try and shlack it or else it will be all over for them. Team 3D has selected Joe to baton the ball over. They are

It All Started In Chem Class...

playing towards the sun. I don't understand this move, but I'm sure they must have a reason for it. And Joe slams the Spaceball, sending it way up into the air, and back to the other team's Abyss, where it will rest until picked up by the team with possession.

"And Hwango, the captain grabs the Spaceball, and immediately sets up for a flying line assault. This is simply where all five of them line up like football players, and just hit whatever comes too close. But, Team 3D immediately sets up in front and behind. Uh-oh, how will the Asian team take this? Oh, that's how. They are now spinning around like the hands on a clock, spinning incredibly fast, and also knocking over the other team! They continue, ever closer to the opposing Abyss.

"But wait, during their spinning hand trick, they overlooked the fact that the other team wasn't complete. The captain, Jim Stupehsmall, was not present when the rest of his team was hit. He is still nowhere to be found! As they near the edge of the Abyss, the team's boards are turning crazy and leading them all over the arena floor. There is only one way to activate the board mess-up switch, and that is internally. As they are taken on a wild ride about the space arena, the rest of the opponents seem to have recovered. They come around, and begin to circle the man with the Spaceball. Like Hwango, he has a long name, and simply goes by Blinkana. He has the Spaceball, but has no control over his board! The other team is flying behind and, but slowly, they are moving up. They have cut him off from his own team. They are circling around him, waiting for the right moment," the announcer said.

Jim waited in the Abyss. He didn't know what was going on above him, out where the action was. He just knew that he had accomplished his goal. He messed up their boards. He would soon have to go back out. He had to wait for the call from Keno, the call that would tell him they had shlacked it. Everything the team did reflected on not only the coach, but Jim especially. If they went to the finals, it would make Jim look good. If they lost, it would make Jim look bad. It was important that he win this match.

Steve was still circling around Blinkana. He was supposed to be the one to shlack the other team. Everyone would obviously expect Keno to do it. That's why Keno wouldn't do it. Steve was fast, but not very good with his hands. He checked his watch. Two minutes left. He suddenly shorted a jet on his board, causing it to falter, just barely. Everyone noticed, of course. This was as planned, so long as the other team didn't know *why* he did it. Everyone else closed in just slightly. He had to drop his baton. It was part of the plan. He dropped it, throwing it more so. The guy slowed down, out of courtesy. *Perfect,* Steve thought. *Time to hit him right on the caps.* He picked up his hammer and then switched up his board just enough that he ran into Blinkana, slamming his baton into his kneecaps. He hunched over, and Steve grabbed the Spaceball. He tossed it lightly to Big Man, the team's heavy hitter.

Big Man had to earn his name. He was the muscle of the team. Keno was small and fast. Big Man was quite the opposite. Keno took off from the instant that Steve's board has faltered. He was already in position to receive the Spaceball. Big Man took the ball in one hand and the baton in the other. He checked to see that his remaining two teammates had him flanked. He hit the ball as hard as he could.

The announcer noticed every little thing, also. "And Steve of Team 3D seems to be having board trouble. He dropped his baton! That move seemed almost intentional. At the same time, Keno speeds off towards the other Abyss. I don't know what they've got up their sleeve, but I'm loving it! Steve slams the knees of the other team's player Blinkana. He grabs the Spaceball and throws it to the man solely known as 'Big Man.' Big Man slams the Spaceball with his baton. It soars across to the waiting hands of Keno. So that's what they were planning. Incredible strategy! I've never seen anything quite like it before. And Keno takes off, with no one near to bother him! I love this sport!"

Jim got the call on his intercom. They had gained control of the Spaceball. He gave the order to send it to Keno. Everything was going perfectly. The Asian Bullet soared toward the Abyss in which he waited. The other team had no chance now. He heard

It All Started In Chem Class... 41

the engines of Keno's board roaring as he came closer. He rose, ready to take care of it. Suddenly, he realized it wasn't Keno to greet him. It was the other team.

The announcer was going crazy. "I don't believe it! The Spaceball has somehow escaped from Keno's grasp! The other team has it, and is now heading towards their own Abyss! I don't understand it. But what's this? The captain of Team 3D is coming up from the opposing Abyss. I'm sure he's less than happy about who came out to meet him!"

Jim heard the announcer in the back of his helmet. He couldn't agree more. And the site that depressed him the most was the site of the Spaceball held by the brother of Hwango, Zennogon. He took the hits with pleasure. He was focused on two things—the watch on his wrist, and the Spaceball. He watched, as his team came in along the ground. He said to them through gritted teeth so as not to let the other team see, "Back off. I'll handle it." He knew they would advance, but not attempt to take the Spaceball. He slowly drew out his baton, but instead of hitting the person with the Spaceball, he hit the people to Zennogon's left and right. He then unbuckled the board, and used it to hit Zennogon over the head, and then catch the Spaceball.

"Jim starts off with a defensive hit to his front-left and front-right. He then smacks Zennogon over the head with his own board, catching the Spaceball! Half the other team is dazed, so Jim takes off, flying through space. This match has only one minute remaining! I doubt if Team 3D can score in that time. Out of nowhere comes Hwango. Jim still has options. Right as Hwango attempts to hit him, Jim ducks and speeds off. He throws it; the Spaceball is soaring. It is caught by none other than *Keno*, who is going towards the Abyss. He doesn't have anything to stop him at this point," the announcer said.

Keno liked the way the announcer yelled his name, adding that extra bit of emphasis on it. And he knew they had to try it. Forty-five seconds left, and his teammates were just slightly behind him. Big Man and Trick Boy ran out to the sides. Keno slowed, giving Jim Stupehsmall enough time to pass in front of him, and go to the other side of the Abyss. Now Steve was only one person behind him. Keno set up right in the center of the Abyss, with Jim behind him, Steve in front, Big Man and Trick Boy on his sides. Keno had the most difficult position of all. They only gave it to him because they knew he could. Now all he had to do was wait for instructions from Jim. He watched Trick Boy as he made several front flips on his board, baton outstretched in a bow. Keno laughed. He noticed the other team almost upon them. *Oh well,* he thought, *not my problem.* This was the only advantage of being the middle man. He had total protection from all sides.

Jim knew it was time. "Keno, get ready. Here's the schedule. You to me to Big to Trick to Steve to me to you to me to you to Steve to Big to you to Trick to you to me to you. Let's try that for now. I might improvise along the way, so watch and listen for it."

"It appears as though the team is preparing for a special tactic called the five-man free-for-all. This is very difficult to pull off, and is hard to follow. Four men each position themselves along one side of the Abyss. One man, in this case, the Bullet, will stand in the middle. The team will volley it back and forth from man to man to man, until the Spaceball begins to realize where to go, and speeds up the process. The idea is that the other team will be completely baffled by this. It apparently is working, seeing as the other team is standing around trying to understand what exactly is going on. I suppose this broadcast is helping them out, but who cares? This is Spaceball, ladies and gentlemen!"

Jim was happy. So long as someone scored, he would be happy. The other team was in complete and utter amazement. Jim continued to utter orders to Keno. The ball went so fast, no one was quite sure where it was going until it got there. Everyone did not include Jim. Jim had the next ten seconds played out in his head before they happened. "Okay, the initial shock is wearing off. Steve to Big to Steve to Trick to Keno to me to Trick. Lock in reflectors," Jim ordered. It was hard to give normal advice while also giving the directions regarding passing

It All Started In Chem Class...

Keno checked his watch. Still ten seconds left. Time seemed to drag on, due in part to the fact that Keno had to hit the ball close to twenty times in a single second. The ball kicked in its own thrusters to move even faster. Keno looked again. Three seconds left.

Jim said, "Do it, Keno."

Keno did it. "Okey dokey," he said. He hit the Spaceball right down. He won the game for the second night in a row. "Thanks Jim!" he shouted, unable to hide his exuberance.

"Pleasure is all mine, Keno," Jim replied, laughing, "The pleasure is all mine."

"Ladies and gentlemen, you have just witnessed an upset, with Team 3D beating Team DOG one to nothing within regulation time. They started off by losing the coin toss, but still managed to win with an incredible display of the five-man free-for-all. An incredible display by Keno, the Asian Bullet, and Jim the 3D Captain. Incredible display by the entire team. They made quite apparent how much this title means to them. Let's hope we see more of the same in the next game. This is Patrick Noble, saying stick around for our next game! We will now have a brief intermission, so that you can go buy food. I mean, so you can recover from the excitement. And also so our team can recover from its last match. Anyway, this is Patrick Noble, saying a temporary good-bye, good bye."

Jim was exhausted. Doing a five-man free-for-all was a tiring method of winning. They had half an hour to rest and go over the plays for the next game. The concept behind this was that if you were good enough to skip round one of the double-header, you would have more time to rejuvenate. But Jim saw it as an opportunity, because they were already in that mind-set. As they were using the full-body muscle massage machines that were in the arena, Jim put up a holographic configuration of the team executing a new stunt that had never been tried before.

It was invented by Spaceball analysts to test the skills of a team. With turf and mines, it would be next to impossible. Jim would have the hardest role in it, so it was justifiable. The trick didn't even have a name. "Okay team, this is gonna be hard. It's never been done before. The obstacles increase the chance of it not working. It could cost us the game. Anyone who doesn't want to try it, leave now. I can replace you," Jim said. No one moved. "Alright. Here's how it works. I start off by turfing it," Jim started. Turfing was just another word for ground skidding. "Now, everyone else will go behind me in the cloud of dust and dirt. Anyone tries to tailgate us, they get hit. I'll go through first and memorize the location of the mines. I'll tell you so you can avoid them. This is called anti-tailgating. Now, to really throw them off-guard, I'm gonna toss the Spaceball to Steve, who will be on my right. Steve, you get it right to Big Man on my left. Big Man to Keno, my far right, and then from Keno back to Tricks over next to Big. Now, Tricks is gonna switch it up with Keno, doing a Turf-X. This is gonna confuse them even more. Now, we all slow down, giving me a few seconds to spin in place, creating a huge whirlwind. I plan to do this near a space mine, so that, well, you get what happens, right? They'll try to shlack Keno, because we've used him so much. But, Keno's not gonna have the Spaceball. I'm gonna start swerving around at this point, to really screw them up. Man, this is gonna be fun. What are your opinions?"

    Big Man spoke up. "Sounds like fun. But do you think we can do it? I mean, this is kinda hard isn't it?"

    "Exactly. Look, I've put up with a pretty bad team. We had to work and we worked hard to get here. I want people to say, 'That is a great team! They had their losing streak, but they are the best team, and they earned that championship.' That's what I want people to say about us. I want to show them we don't win on luck. This will show them that. This will show them that we can outmaneuver the other people. We have to show them in this match the opposite of what our record says. Now, we got a little time. Repeat this in your head. Over and over and over again. Is there any question?" Jim yelled the last question, even though it was rhetorical.

It All Started In Chem Class...   45

They all answered in unison, *"Yes, sir, Captain sir!"* They all could care less. Steve could care less. All he cared about was the massage. *Whoa, this feels great,* he thought. The muscle massage was specially designed to rejuvenate in one-half hour. Steve was already feeling perfect. But the massage wasn't even over. He stared at that diagram, memorized it. The problem was the diagram didn't know where they placed the mines. That had a lot to do with it. Steve didn't care, though. He had an easy part. Follow Jim, avoid the mine. Over and over again he thought it to himself. He was completely ready. Suddenly, the massage machine was done. It was time for the announcements.

Chris watched everything, through the convenience of the little monitor that he and his team were privy to, sitting in box seats.Air conditioned, with catered food, and a monitor from which they watched the pre-game 3D talk. Chris noticed Steve. Steve seemed to go into a trance. He seemed to be thinking the same thing over and over. *Must be a simple play,* Chris thought, chuckling. They watched the play for half an hour. Then, the announcer, who was positioned in a "safe probe" high in the arena began his announcements.

"Welcome, one and all, to the second game of our double-header. This is the first EVER Senior Spaceball Finals. Tonight, we match up two of the best teams. They are Team Alpha-Beta-Gamma a.k.a. Team 123, the team with absolutely *zero* losses as of yet. In this case, they could be out with only one loss. Here they come, out on to the field, *Team Alpha-Beta-Gamma!"* The crowd was roaring for the favored team. The odds were 6:1 in favor of the team. He continued, "Now, please welcome, *Team Delta-Delta-Delta!"* The crowd was quieter but still very loud.

"And now, the referee is joined by the team captains for the ceremonial coin toss. This game, we are using a special coin. The heads side bears the image of a Spaceball, while the tails side bears the image of two helmets, one emblazoned with the bright triangles, in all three dimensions I might add, and the other emblazoned with the letters ABG, and the logo, 'It's just that easy.' The 3D captain, Jim a.k.a. the Jersey Rocket, will be making the call for tonight's game. Let's listen in," Pat Noble said.

The referee took his cue. "Tonight is the first ever Spaceball Senior Finals. We are using this special coin for the coin toss. Jim, you get to make the call. Call it in the air!"

"Heads!" Jim shouted, so everyone could here. The coin seemed to take forever to come back down. Jim felt like it was going in slow motion.

Chris watched the coin toss only a few feat away. His box seat was close to the action. This was one advantage of playing the game. The pizza he was eating was another. He felt like the coin toss took a really long time, but at least he knew why. He had a direct holophone link to the announcer. He called him up. "Hey, Pat. What's with the coin? Don't lie, I know that you know. So tell me," Chris said.

"Chris, I would have thought that you could figure that out," he replied.

"Yeah, I figured they did the helium injection," Chris said, sighing.

"Yep, you are correct. I'm still not sure why they do that, but hey man, the announcements are about to start. As soon as that stupid thing lands," Patrick said, frustration in his voice. The coin came down, landing upon three small triangles and 3D letters of ABG. The Spaceball was facing up. The announcer took it up again. "And Team 3D has won the coin toss! They choose to take the Spaceball. This should be quite a game. This is Pat Noble, saying welcome back from an exciting match between Team 3D and Team DOG, with Team 3D coming out on top. Final score for that, one to nothing. So, a couple of tricky moves and one score later, Team 3D is out on top. But I know you want me to shut up, so I will. Oh never mind, here is some pure homegrown *Spaceball action!*"

Team 3D took their cue. They set up in their normal star-formation and began passing the Spaceball. This move was legal, until the team crossed halfway. This got the ball up to speed. Now they took off, and immediately set up for a Suicidal Slapstick

It All Started In Chem Class... 47

move. They began to hit each other. The plan didn't work as well as Jim had hoped. The other team caught on quickly. They abused the move as Jim had hoped they wouldn't realize they could. Unfortunately, he was wrong. Every time they started to hit each other, the other team double-teamed one of their players. He was frustrated. The only move he had lined up next was the hardest move ever attempted. And they would have to make it work. He didn't have any new tricks up his sleeve. He gave the command. "Get ready for the move," he told them with his best, deepest command voice.

"Cap, what are we gonna call it?"

"The X-Ecutioner's Axe," Jim told Steve.

"Genius."

"Yeah, but we can't start it yet. We have to start off with a spinning bar. I'll take middle. Ready? After this, we move right to a five-man free-for-all. Keno, you got it?"

"Yeah. My momma didn't raise no fool!" Keno exclaimed, laughing. They went into a spin-motion, and it was easy. The difficult part was what came next. They spun around and around. This left them quite dizzy, and doing the next move was very difficult.

"Doing what is fast becoming their signature move, Team 3D is performing the five-man free-for-all after what is known as a space hazard. This leaves them dizzy, and should provide nothing more than a great show. Let's see how it goes. Ooh, they are executing the free-for-all with ease. I don't know how they do it; I just know they do. I wonder if this is how they intend to score, or even win the finals. On the other hand they could just be stalling," he said.

Keno knew they'd be coming right for him. He was ready. He was centered over the Abyss and under a space mine. He figured they couldn't mess with him now. But he was ready anyway. He was still a little dizzy, but that wasn't about to stop him. Following Jim's instructions, he spun the opposite direction in place. Jim said this did something for an equilibrium or some such thing. All he knew was that he wasn't very dizzy anymore.

The five-man free-for-all was going well enough. He fended off attacks on all sides. The announcer was right, Keno thought. They were stalling in the biggest way. This was all part of the plan.

Chris watched them, his eyes squinted in keen concentration. He knew they were stalling. He knew they would attempt to do whatever they would call that really tough move. But he also knew it would take five minutes, tops. So he knew they were just stalling. It was fun to watch, though. Chris thought that they should just score now. But then again, winning on a signature move makes people think of a team as unoriginal. Chris didn't want that. He told Jim via his special com system, "Hey man, when you gonna do it?"

"Probably soon as I have time. I like the stall though," Jim said.

"Yeah, but they will get the Spaceball. Dude, pull out. If you do it right, the move will level the playing field, and they won't have a chance," Chris replied.

"Not necessarily. I'm gonna take it in four minutes," Jim said, checking his watch. There were six minutes left. Two minutes would give him all the time he needed. He relayed the message to the rest of his team. They all agreed. Four minutes they kept up that move.

"I'm getting tired. I wanna see some *action!* Come on teams, show me something! I'm growing gray hairs here! Oh? What's this? Yes! At last, some show from Tricks, on Team 3D. He is now hitting the ball inverted, and also spinning around. Ah, this is the essence of Trick Dude. Oh, what's this? It appears as though two men from the other team, Team 123, have infiltrated the maneuver! And they *take the Spaceball! This is what the sport's all about!*" Patrick paused to take a drink of water.

Chris sighed, forlorn. He knew this would happen. He warned them. He told them not to. And all in vain. They had gone on too long. He knew his team would have to get them out of it. They knew how to get the ball. He spoke quickly into the microphone in his helmet. "Okay, this is gonna be tricky. See the guy with the Spaceball? Here's what you have to do. Find the guy

It All Started In Chem Class...

closest to him. Get Tricks, Biggie, and you on him. Keep a distance; don't be obvious. You don't want them to know you're three steps ahead. Now, send Keno and Steve to the guy with the Spaceball. Keep an eye out in case someone comes up from the other side. Once Keno and Steve get there, have them beat him until he either gives it up or passes to your man. If he does either, well, you get the picture," Chris said.

"I love that rule," Jim said in reply.

"The no-foul rule?"

"The help-from-other-related-teams rule," Jim answered. He relayed the commands to the rest of the team. No one had any complaints. Chris coached them through it. He told them when to back off, when to come in, and other things like that. It went very well. They made the steal justas they neared the Abyss. Keno hit a beauty to the other person's kneecap, while Steve socked him in the gut. He used fisting, which was hitting with a fist and not a baton.

Patrick resumed his announcements, saying, "It appears as though Team 3D is not trying to take it at the moment. Keno and Steve, however, are setting up around the man with the Spaceball. The other three, for some reason that must make sense to them, are following some other person on the other team. They near their own Abyss, and Keno slams the person's kneecap, while Steve simultaneously fists his stomach. He immediately throws the Spaceball to the first person he sees, who is the same person that Team 3D has been guarding! *They take the Spaceball!*"

Chris smiled. They did it right. He watched, enveloped in the game, as they turned around and came back to the Team 123 goal. *Time for the biggie,* he thought.

"And it appears as though they are about to attempt what is only known as Analyst Move #24. This move was created to practice. The analysts who came up with it had no idea it could decide the outcome of a match, the Finals, no less! This move should be great! The space mines and turf increase the probability of its going completely wrong. That makes it even more fun! The move is hard to perform, anyway. But with debris, it is very difficult. Seeing as it was only invented yesterday, I'm sure they have not practiced it as of yet. The captain, Jim, has started off by turfing, which is running his board along the ground, sending dirt and debris into the space. This makes following him very difficult. But, according to the move, it is required for his team to follow him, which they are doing."

    Jim was telling them where to go. "Mine on the left, whoa, duck Steve! Keno, swerve left. Tricks, mine field dead ahead. Keep formation! Okay team, time to mix it up a little bit. Steve, get set up, because I'm about to have to dodge a mine," Jim said. Steve sidled up alongside him, making the pass simple. Steve slowed down, so he could complete his part of the job. He threw it to Big Man, on the other side of Jim. Big Man took his cue, and served it to Keno. Keno waited a little while before sending it to Tricks, who was doing aerials in place. Tricks took it and waited for his cue. "Alright, Tricks, Keno, make it happen!" Jim yelled at them through his microphone.

    "As the rest of the team enters the debris along the ground, they all begin to go through nose facing up, creating an even field of debris. As they enter, Jim is dead center, with Steve and Keno on his right, Big Man and Tricks on his left. They are doing an incredible job of swerving around the various obstacles. It has to be hard to navigate in there. Team 123 won't give up without a fight, though. They are entering the debris field, apparently sending two people ahead to show them where the mines are. This technique appears to be working; I barely make them out going through the mine field. Ooh, the front men take a bad hit on several mines, but that really helps point it out for the others. Two members of Team 3D seem to be doing a Turf-X, which is where two people, both turfing, come right at each other. One lifts up while the other pushes down, creating a perfect X in the arena. It is done, and they have switched sides completely. They are nearing the Abyss, with Team 123 hot on their tails. This means that soon they will have to come out of the mine fields, and face whatever is behind, or in front of them. What's this? Another Turf-X? This is strange. Why would they do that?"

It All Started In Chem Class...

Chris wondered the same thing. What was Jim thinking? He decided to find out. "Jim, what's going on? I can't see anything," he said.

"I just realized that after having Tricks and Keno do the switch, they would go after Keno, on the right side. They play with the announcements off," Jim said. "So if they didn't hear that, they wouldn't know."

"But what if they did? Jim, do it one more time. They do know what's going on, trust me. Once more. The third time's the charm," Chris said. Jim did just as he said. Now they were both flying in their original positions, Tricks living up to his name, and Keno his.

"Another X makes it three. I guess the message is 'Three strikes you're out at the Spaceball game.' As they come out of the turfed area, it's obvious they are in the same pattern that they used going in. The other team has created a semi-circle around Keno, who is trying his best to fend them off. But he doesn't seem to have the Spaceball! Tricks is going to put it in! He hits it right to Big Man, who hands it to Jim. This is Jim's big moment. But one of his engines seems to be faulting out! He had a top of the line board, but something has gone wrong, terribly wrong! He's now swerving, out of control! I doubt anyone will be able to stop him from his fate. With his one motor going strong, he is going around in circles. The force stops him from getting his baton to defend himself from attacks! This has to be a manufacturer's problem. But in Spaceball, you know what they say: 'It's the manufacturer's problem, not yours, so *get over it!*' His vision is blurred, obviously, and he tries to throw the Spaceball to Steve, but it is caught by none other than the other team's captain, Gwenfanio, who takes it to the 3D goal and puts it in, winning the game in regulation time," Patrick said. "This has been one incredible night, first an upset by Team 3D, then a stunning win by the favorites, Team 123, in the last seconds, due to a motor malfunction. This is Patrick Noble, saying great games, good food, great time, good night! Good night!"

CHAPTER 7: THE PROJECTS

Chris, Rich, John, Bob, and Jordan went back to their dorm. They were all exhausted, after a full hour of Spaceball. They still had to practice, as their own Finals were only two weeks away. Chris had a lot of new moves in store for them, but now he just wanted some sleep. They met up with the rest of the teams from Delta-Delta-Delta, doing what should have been a victory run through the school. But, do to a faulty motor in a perfectly good board, they had lost. Chris couldn't complain. The team had done it all right. Nothing *should* have stopped them. But that one little motor did. It made Chris think of how something so small and seemingly insignificant could mean the difference between champions and another regular old team. After he got back to the dorm, Chris changed into something comfortable, and fell asleep instantly, as did the rest of his room. They weren't really that troubled by the loss, but it still hurt them.

"So, what are you guys doing for the weekend?" Chris spoke as he yawned. He glanced outside, still amazed by the view of Earth from in orbit. He looked to the US, his former home.

"I have to build a ship. My teacher is *insane*," Bob said.

"What's so hard about that?" Rich cocked an eyebrow.

"Well, can you build an R/C shuttle that can land in Houston, Texas?"

"Nope," Rich replied.

"Okay then, that's the assignment. I got a fine budget. I don't see how this will benefit us, though," Bob said, sighing.

"Well, where do you get that stuff, anyway? What's this for? EEU?" Rich asked, referring to the things necessary to operate the R/C shuttle.

"Radio Shack. And also, that's what it's for," Bob replied, smiling. So, they all flew over to the local Radio Shack.

"An antenna that can operate in Houston from the station?" The man behind the counter said. "Are you insane?"

"No, it's for a project," Bob said.

It All Started In Chem Class...

"Yeah, we got those in the back. What is the purpose of this project, anyway?"

"You don't know how long I've been working on that one!" Bob followed the guy to the back room, where their top-quality supplies were kept. They did it this way to prevent the most expensive merchandise from being stolen. Despite the high-tech security, theft was quite common. The clerk handed Bob a receiver, a battery, a radio, and a remote control. The price was in the thousands of dollars. "This should do it. These are top quality parts. I think you can get an A on whatever it is you're doing. What kind of motors and such are you using? They have to use Superfuel, right?"

"I think that's how I'll do it. I guess I don't really have much choice. I'd rather do it that way than making those *huge* cylinders. That would take some cash from my own pocket, and we both know that's not happening! Besides, those things are way too big. Where would I get the Superfuel?"

"Not sure. You can probably get it at the Grin Gas. It sells premium, and lots of others," he said. "Tell them Pete sent you. They can give you some nice stuff. You could most likely fit it in a box thirty centimeters square, two centimeters in depth. They have the best stuff ever over there. Oh well, here's your change. Wow, they did give you some money, huh?"

"Yeah, I need the receipt. That's how they know we didn't blow it," Bob answered, referring to the large funds he had received. He took the package and left.

It was fairly small, but it did have an incredible range. Bob looked at it. As they walked to Grin, They talked about their classes.

"Dude, Earth History is so boring! I mean, maybe it's me, but I don't care how many countries helped build this place! All I know is they did a good job of it!" John sighed, knowing the teachers wouldn't buy that. Then, he saw the same teacher who taught them those useless facts.

"Really," the teacher said. "I once had the same opinion on school," he said, sighing. "Then, I found something out.

Throughout your life, people are going to ask you the exact same things we are telling you now! That's why it's important. One day, you may make fun of someone who's Russian, and they might remind you that half of the force that *built* this place was from Russia! If we make fun of them, we get hurt. Now do you appreciate what we teach you?"

"To a larger extent. Thanks, Mr. Jones, we really appreciate it!"

"Sure. I try to inspire my students. One day, you will thank me for this," he said. Chris and the rest walked into the Grin Gas Station. Bob acted like he owned the place.

"Yeah, uh, you know Pete? We're close, man, we're like that," he said, crossing his fingers. "He told me to come down here and get the stuff. I'm making a project for class, and he said you'd have the kind of fuel I'd need."

"Superfuel? That stuff is strong, I'm telling ya! I wouldn't recommend it unless you plan to make something that's going straight to Earth," Tim behind the counter said.

"That's the assignment. How do you think it will help the world we live in?"

"Well, it certainly will make our stocks go higher," Tim said. "It is cheaper than sending an entire archaic shuttle down there. Okay, this should do it. I'll give you twice the amount you need, for a return journey. I'm sure you've got the money for it, right?"

"Yeah. Thanks." They walked back to the room. Everyone else did their homework while Bob got the motors and stuff. John was working on a new form of acid. It was supposed to eat through certain materials, and be completely safe to others.

"Here we go. This is resistant to glass and rubber, but it eats straight through steel. This will be awesome for melting down pistols. Just carry it in a rubber-coated glass vial. Think it will get an A?" He poured it into a glass vial, and coated that with rubber. He recorded his results with a look of satisfaction.

"Does it go through homework, by any chance?" Rich grinned. "I've got a killer report to do, but oh well. It's in Matter

It All Started In Chem Class…

Teleportation. Title has to be 'Why is matter teleportation important to me?' I don't know why it's important," he said as he hit two buttons, popping up a sheet of plastic and a laser-point pen to start writing.

"Hey, there's something right there! You just zap your pen and plastic right to you," Chris commented.

"I guess you're right. I do like the pizza button, and the remote button. Man, once you get started the ideas just keep coming!" While he wrote, Chris began looking at a 3D hologram of a spaceship he had designed. He had to go over it, examining every detail. If it looked good to his teacher, he would see it produced. Then, he would test drive it to the edge of the solar system and back again. If it had even one design flaw, he might die on his test drive. He threw on a couple of plasma cannons, just in case. He had bad steering, so he used those to hit anything smaller than a moon and blast it out of his way. Weekends were when Chris and the rest had the most homework.

"Nice job, Chris. I'm sure you want me to draw in some electronic controls, right?" Jordan majored in Space Ship Electronics, which made everything Chris's class designed work.

"Yeah, would you? No offense, but this stuff isn't even in my text book!" Chris was still looking at it, checking for even a millimeter of an imperfection. He saw one instance of a slightly crooked tile. This meant that his ship would be shredded if it passed too close to a planet. He took out his etcher tool, which created the hologram, and fixed the imperfection. He enlarged the model so he could walk inside of it. It seemed to be in order, except for the fact that it lacked every sort of electronic device possible. He called Jordan in, and showed him. Jordan got a feel for it and what it would need.

"Very nice. This gives me a lot of room to work with. I could put in the basic computer system. I could throw in an HTV, pizza maker, other necessities. In fact, I'll get you luxuries, my friend. My assignment was to make the most hybrid electronics system ever! If I make this for you, I'll get an 'A' for sure! I mean, making this is one thing, but if I install it too, no one else will stand a chance!" Chris smiled, thinking of his hybrid system. He knew Jordan could make anything. He expected nothing less than a pizza maker, an HTV, which meant either Holographic Television or Hybrid Television. Chris and his friends either called it Hybrid or just HTV. He would have an internal satellite, which could send him hundreds of channels without damaging his flying ability. He was gonna be in for a trip of probably a full month or two. He added the rockets, Superfuel cells, batteries, and smoothed over the edges. It looked perfect.

"What do you think?" C

"A," John replied.

"A," Rich answered.

"A," Jordan chimed in. They all agreed it was good work. It would take six or seven month to build, and at least a month to try it. This was his biggest project. He had been working on it for most of the year. This would decide whether he passed or failed the class. He had to miss his last month of classes to test it out. This was one of the reasons many people signed up for the class. Many changed majors after finding out the chances of surviving DSD.

Bob came back with a large crate filled with building materials. They went to help him unload. Soon, each roommate was busy doing his own project. Bob had the motors, controls, and materials. He employed slave labor to help him. That labor presented itself in the form of his falcon helping him. *Fenix* cooperated, despite his loathe of work. Fenix helped weld the frame, attach the internals, and bring Bob food. "Fenix, you're a lifesaver," Bob said quitegraciously.

Chris's project was due the Monday after he finished it. He stayed up almost as late as Bob did on that Saturday. He worked until 0100 hours that night. He found innumerable things that were off fractionally, yet still problematic enough to send it straight to disaster on some foreign planet.

Rich got to sleep around midnight. He had finished his entire 10,000-word essay on why he thought matter teleportation was important. His pet, Bigpaw, helped him think. He zapped him

It All Started In Chem Class... 57

in to feed him and zapped him out for a break or for being annoying. He had never realized how much he took teleportation for granted. After finishing, he used his desk-bed teleportation device.

John had strengthened his acid, and also made a diluted formula. He made them each a different color, so he could tell them apart. He had to get an "A" on this, because his specialty was acids. Everyone had to do well in general chemistry, and even better in their specialty. He went to sleep around eleven, before his friends.

Jordan was up all night, building a complete electronics system from scratch. It was hard, but he had nothing else to do. He first got a complete computer system to control the basic functions of the ship. He then had to add advanced chips to control the steering and weaponry. He added latches for the fall-away parts, just in case. Then, he began to equip the luxuries. He put on an HTV, with digital recording. He threw in a stereo, a pizza maker, and a refrigerator. He added a D3D player, which had movies etched onto minidisks in 3D code, so they appeared in all three dimensions. He put on so many appliances; the ship even had its own personal kitchen. Of course, nothing could be installed until the rest of the ship was done. He went to sleep around four the next morning.

The next day proved very uneventful. They sat around and watched HTV all day, taking a break for an in-space church service. Chris asked, "When is the Super Bowl? How many weeks away is it?"

Rich replied, "About three weeks."

"Wow, is it really past Christmas and everything? Where does the time go?"

"Well, you sleep quite a lot, Chris," Bob said. "You probably slept through most of it. Wait, no, I remember now; you got a new visor and some cash for Christmas. You stayed up till oh-six-hundred on New Year's Eve."

"Oh yeah, the memories are flooding me now," Chris said.

CHAPTER 8: THE CHASE

Monday brought meteor showers like solid rain. The meteors rocked the ship, but didn't hurt it. Every one of Chris's friends had classes on Monday. They each had their majors on Monday, Wednesday, and Friday. They went to their required classes on Tuesday and Thursday. John was happy about the shower. "Woohoo! The Chem shuttle is delayed for an entire hour! Less class for me today!"

"I'm in Deep-Space Design. That means our ships are loaded with armor to handle mine fields. I'm running late. I had to pick the one that gets me out a month!"

"Oh well, more sleep time for John!" John went to bed laughing. The others got their set of books ready. They each had two books in their major.

"Well, I have full-day sessions today," Chris said, "So I have to leave soon, 0830 hours. See you guys later." Everyone had one full-day session and two half-day sessions. They had the core classes in between. Bob and everyone else liked this setup, because they enjoyed their majors more than History, Math, Science, and Literature, which were their core classes. They were also the boring classes. Everyone aboard the space station, save the nerds, hated core classes. They were the classes with the lowest approval rating of all seven classes. Their seventh class was an elective and was somewhat enjoyable.

"Excuse me, someone open up this dorm room! This is the police!"

"Rich, you wanna get that?" Bob yawned as he spoke.

"Great, give *me* the police," he grumbled as he answered the door. "Yes, gentlemen, can we help you in any way?"

"We are looking for someone by the name of Chris Johnson. He is the prime suspect in a cheating scandal. Is he in here?" As the policeman spoke, Chris hopped on his board, grabbed his spaceship model, and slipped out the door into space, wearing his suit with a full oxygen tank.

It All Started In Chem Class... 59

"Uh, sir, if you don't mind me asking, what exactly are the charges against him?" Rich knew he had to stall until Chris got to his class.

"He has been charged by a staff personwith rigging a Spaceball event," the officer explained sternly.

"How could he, hypothetically, have rigged the event? I do know Chris, and I doubt he would be smart enough to do something like that," Rich said, trying not to be obvious.

"We think that he clogged Jim's rockets. Jim is the captain of the Spaceball Team 3D. We believe that he bet on the team, and then rigged the game to lose, in money laundering. We think that someone gave him something, and that he rigged the game to pay the person in an inconspicuous way. Now, is he here or isn't he?"

"Officer, do you have any warrants for search or arrest? What is the basis of these warrants? What evidence do you have against him?"

"We know that someone on the inside put foam inside his pipe, to fault an engine. This foam was timed to explode just as Jim was going to win the game. Only someone on the inside could have done this. We know that Chris was in close contact with the team. For this reason, he is our prime suspect in the money-laundering case. *Is he here?*"

"Sir, I mean no offense to you or your investigators, but how do you know that it was time-release foam? Perhaps Jim left it out in a meteor shower and a meteor fell inside it, and it took that long to get into the actual motor. Or perhaps another team, jealous of their success, clogged it to get rid of them," Bob suggested, with a grin across his face. Chris was in his next class by now. At least, he thought he was.

Chris sped around the Space Station, trying to get to his class. Suddenly, he saw something very unsettling. There were two police shuttles tailing him. He had just installed a new feature on his board, for which he was thankful, as he turned it on. It switched fuel sources, sending out deep, black smoke. He swerved, in and out, up and down, to avoid the shuttles. Just as the fuel was running out, and the smoke thinning, he ducked into a tunnel, hidden by a special holographic projector, he made it to his class. He had a secret space right under his seat. As he settled in, he called Rich on his holophone. "Dude, thanks for stalling. What's up with them? What are they after me for?"

"Clogging Jim's engine," Rich said, the police now off in search of a Chemistry shuttle, where he informed them that Chris would be.

"Was it even clogged?"

"They said it was."

"And they had a warrant?"

"Yeah. They didn't find anything. They were looking for time-release foam."

"I don't even have any of that! I'm fresh out," Chris exclaimed quietly. "Hey, man, I gotta go; I need to call Jim and see what's up with his board."

"Alright. See ya later," Rich said, closing his holophone on his way to Matter Teleportation. Holophones were the communication of the future. Instead of giving you someone's voice to listen to, it made a complete, three dimensional image of the person right before your eyes. This prevented prank calls to some extent, and were the greatest form of communication ever invented. He had less than twenty seconds to get there, when he remembered his matter transporter would get him there in a quarter or the time. He zapped himself in, just in time.

"Yeah, Jim, sorry about this, I'm sure you're hard at work," Chris said.

"Not quite. Anyway, whatcha need?"

"Check your exhaust pipes, and tell me what's in there. They're trying to say I was involved in cheating, setting a time-release foam ball in your exhaust pipes. I just got away from the cops. If Rich hadn't stalled, I would've been done for," Chris said.

"Okay, checking now. There's not a foam ball. In fact, there are the charred remains of chewing gum in here. That's odd," he said in a puzzled tone.

"What? It's chewing gum? That is weird," Chris said, equally puzzled.

"Yeah, I would have used bubble gum, as it tends to be thicker than chewing gum. Steve, run me a diagnostic test on this gum!" Steve was a senior majoring in Chemistry, specialty in testing. "Steve said it appears to be Double Mint. Someone on the other team must have done it. If the cops come, I'll tell them everything about this, while Tricks gets over to Team 123's dorm and looks for gum. I'll keep you posted. And uh, the teacher's about to ask you a question," Jim finished

"Thanks. See you later, man!" Chris hung up his holophone and threw himself up into his chair, right as the teacher came by.

"Chris, can you please tell me what happens to a spaceship if a tile is one millimeter off?" the teacher asked

"If it is entering into a decent atmosphere, the tile will be ripped off, bringing the rest of the ship down with it. The ship will be destroyed, and the crew killed. If an asteroid were to hit that tile, it would rip open the ship, creating a vacuum and sucking everything out, killing everyone. If an asteroid hit any other part of the ship, it would be knocked off-balance, sending it off-course and probably destroying the ship. Small imperfections can destroy the entire ship, sir."

"Very good answer, Chris. Have you designed your ship?"

"Why of course, sir. It is due today, isn't it?"

"Yes, and I don't have yours. Do you have it with you?"

"Right here, sir." Chris pulled out the small disk that kept his design on it and handed it to the teacher. Then, he felt his holophone vibrate, notifying him of a call. He knew it was from Jim. He switched to silent mode, which read his lips, so the teacher wouldn't know he was using his phone in class, which was against school policy.

"Bad news, man," Jim said. "They think that I gave you the money you supposedly laundered. They want to hold you in prison until there is strong proof supporting our theory of the other team's doing it. Those coppers really hate you. Can you get out of there? Try the old 'gotta barf quick' excuse. Anyway, they might be back, so I'll catch you later." Chris didn't have to say anything.

"Oh, teacher, I don't feel too good! I gotta go now!" Chris ran out into the hall, where his board and spacesuit were waiting. He saw the police running towards him. He sped through door into space. They were right behind him. Chris jumped onto his board, and took off. The police didn't have a way to travel in space. Chris was well aware of this, which is why he acted in such a rash manner. He knew the cop shuttles would come around soon. But he sped off, taking the time advantage for all it was worth.

"Sir, are you Chris Johnson?" He heard them using a telecom system to speak directly into his radio that he had on his Spaceboard. He was going to toy with them.

"Who? I can't hear you!" He sprayed hair spray (he was very concerned about his appearance, and had a bottle of hair spray or gel on him at all times) into the radio. "Ah, you're breaking up. What's that? I can't hear you! Kiss floss in? I'm sorry; I don't follow what you mean. What? I'm sorry; there's a terrible storm out!" Chris turned off his radio, smiling. His story was believable enough. Now he just had to get to safety before their jet power caught up with him. They began firing laser cannons at him. Chris had to do some tricky moves to outmaneuver the shots. Despite his proficiency at flying, Chris got nicked by one of them, but it didn't bleed, so he was fine. Chris was about to make a fast turn around the station. He knew that would throw them off, and give him just enough time to get inside the Spaceball arena, which was unoccupied at the time. Chris flew into a special door used for runaway Spaceballs. He flew in and went straight to the locker rooms.

The police ships had been thrown off by the turn, and saw no signs of Chris Johnson. The officer had no idea what he should do, so he radioed to the headquarters. "This is ship #RPF sector C, car 4. We have lost sign of who we believe to be the fugitive. He cut off his radio, said something about breaking up. What should we do?"

It All Started In Chem Class...

Headquarters answered, "Split up! Find him at all costs! We think he might be involved in the mafia! That's why he was involved in money laundering. It is imperative that we find this man!"

"Sir, yes, sir! We're splitting up now, and leaving the ships," he told the chief. Then, to the rest of his squad, he yelled, "*Split up!* Two of you check that big dome over there! Two of you check that hallway. I'm going for that classroom. Radio in if you find him."

Chris listened to these transmissions via a radio he had "found" aboard the station during a drug raid. Fortunately, he chose the locker room (as his temporary hideout) for a specific reason. It had a secret escape tunnel used by Spaceball players to avoid the press after large games. He ducked out, grabbing an extra can of fuel as he went, and sped off towards the bathrooms.

Once in the hall, he grabbed a second board, which was lighter and had better maneuverability; it was used just for boarding down the halls. It was commonly known as a Hoverboard, since it could be used in gravity fields. He threw on some normal clothes over his special flesh-colored suit. He went out the nearest exit, because he knew the cop cars had been evacuated during their raid inside the school. He went out, and saw that the engine was still running.

Stupid cops, he thought. *Never can do the smart thing.* Chris just slipped in and took off, placing a call to Steve. "Hey, you find that gum? I'm being chased in a police car! No, I'm *in* the police car. Look, I don't really like being an international fugitive here, so can you please find something to clear my name?"

"I'm working on it. The people in this dorm are just leaving for class. And they're gone. Okay, I'm in the room. What's your location?"

"I'm just cruising around the school. I think I see your wing," Chris said.

"Aha! It's a fresh pack of Double Mint with one stick missing! Come by and get me!" Chris went right to Steve, who had on his spacesuit. Steve hopped in the cop shuttle; they turned around, and Chris got out the police radio.

"We now have strong evidence supporting my total and complete lack of involvement. We have found a pack of Double Mint gum, with one stick missing, in the dormitory of the opposing team of the Spaceball finals. This is the same type of gum we found burned on the interior of Jim's board. We ask that you take this into account. We understand that you, officers, have an independent lab doing similar research. I want you to know that the only reason I have been fleeing is that I've been biding my time, waiting for this evidence to surface. I knew that I was wrongfully accused and therefore did whatever was necessary to stay out of prison until my name was cleared. You may have your police vehicle back, under the single condition that I am released and not arrested." Chris finished as the police received a call from their independent lab.

"Sir, it was just as they said. The gum matches the chemical structure of Double Mint exactly," the lab technician said.

"Very well. Let's just put this whole fiasco behind us, shall we? This would look very bad on my record, so just give me back the car, and stay out of trouble, okay?" the officer said in a deep voice, trying to act like he had been in control the whole time

"Okay, we'll do it your way," Chris answered. He and Steve jumped out onto their boards, pulled the car back and went back to their classes.

CHAPTER 9: THE INSPECTION

Chris arrived back in his class, seeing his own design at the front. It was now an hour later, but this class extended forever, it seemed to him.

"Well Chris, the class was critiquing your design," his teacher told him.

"Really? And what do they think of the design?"

"They think the electronics system will need to be extremely complex for this to work properly. How do you plan to cover this electronics need?"

"My friend, Jordan, is a major in Shuttle Electronics. He is planning to provide and install the entire system as part of his final project," Chris answered coolly.

"Ah, very interesting. Is he required to install it? Or is that just a personal favor?"

"He thinks that the installation of said units will help better his grade."

"Very well. Everything else seemed to be in perfect order," the teacher said with a look of defeat. "Construction will begin immediately. I promise it will be ready by the end of the term. Well, the end of our term, anyway. Well, class is dismissed!"

Chris went back to his dorm, checking his watch. It was already 1530 hours. He checked his friend's date book for homework. He didn't have any. He tossed it back to his friend just before getting to his dormitory room.

"How was your trip?" Rich smiled.

"Oh, you know same old same old. I got some good Spaceball practice. Ever tried dodging bullets? Anyway, my name is cleared. So, can we not talk about it?"

"Okay, fine," Rich said, sighing. "My teacher said that I really appreciate the small things, according to my report. I got an 'A' because he said so many people go to bed without thinking about what it would be like to walk the three meters from wherever they are to their bed."

"I got an 'A' on my acid project. Teach said it was quote 'Excellent! The best project I have seen yet!' Really was sorta easy. I don't care though. Now he's making us identify certain forms of acid. I have to identify sulfuric, synthetic, and various other forms of acids. It's hard. I have to know the difference between natural sulfuric and synthetic sulfuric. This is a hard specialty. I'll be at the lab if you need me," John said. The lab was a section of the dorm where John had his acidic ingredients set aside to play with or do projects with. Sometimes, he would be in there for a day or two.

"Chris, when does construction start on the ship?" Jordan seemed impatient to install his electronics.

"Started today. Should be done in six months or so. Is the stuff ready?"

"All I need is a few batteries, and it will be done."

"Great. The whole class critiqued it. They all said it was great, as long as the electronics work."

"They will," Jordan said confidently.

"That's what I'm afraid of," Chris said, laughing. "You might have to go along and show me how it works. By the way, have any of you heard from the dean about that SETI thing?"

"Nope, but I think he's still working on it," Bob answered.

"Okay, that's cool. I'm not gonna worry about it. I just wanted to know. Well, since I don't have any homework, I'm gonna do something I never have the chance to do."

"Go to sleep at 1630 hours?" John grinned, guessing the answer.

"You're smart, man. See you guys tomorrow." Chris yawned and used Rich's teleportation unit to go to bed. This was one reason he loved living in space. He could turn off his light and have total darkness, save a few stars in space. Once his blinds were down, he couldn't even tell the sun was out.

Bob still had to work on his R/C project. It was due on Wednesday, and that was also his next EEU class. He finished it that Monday night. The rest of them had homework too. Rich had to design something that could teleport to a mobile target. That

It All Started In Chem Class...   67

meant making something adhesive so that it would stick to the desired object. It also meant a constantly reconfiguring port on the other end, to assure that whatever was transported did not become part of a statue or something sick like that. His was due Friday. Chris was one of the only people that was able to fall into bed early that night. Jordan, having finished his entire system over the weekend, went to sleep at his normal time of 2000 SST.

The next morning they got up early, planning to pay a visit to the dean's office. They stopped by the Café Probe, getting some much needed sugar in the form of donuts and sodas, and left. They made their way around the halls, looking out for any teachers with insomnia. They saw a light on in the dean's office. They hid around a corner, and listened.

"I'm in charge of the SETI program, and I don't understand how some freshmen ball players are going to help our mission!" Some big shot from SETI had apparently arrived in the middle of the night.

"Listen, I don't really care about *your* mission. We are paying you plenty of cash to do this. I don't want you telling me what to do! I am ultimately in charge of this operation. Is that understood?"

"Yes, sir," the SETI agent replied, sighing. "I didn't mean to undermine your authority by any means, sir. I just didn't see how your choice of freshmen could benefit the experiments we plan to conduct."

"If we just use brainy people, there's no way we'll get the varied results we need. We have to use them for their muscle capacity, not their mental capacity. And also, they happen to be insomniacs," he said.

"Bad news, man! *Run for it!*" John exclaimed quietly. They all took off. Fortunately, Rich brought the smaller, silent Spaceboards, which even worked in normal gravitational fields, such as the one on the space station. These boards were called hoverboards, because they had the ability to hover and defy gravity. They easily made it back into their room without the dean seeing them.

"Oh well, not exactly how I had planned it," Chris said. He pulled out his special heat seeking glasses to see if the dean was coming. He was, alongside the SETI agent. Chris turned on his snore machine, which was a recording of real college kids snoring at that exact hour of the night, designed for perfect reality. The dean knocked. Chris was tense. He knocked again, louder this time. Chris decided to play along. He hit the "wake-up" button on his snore machine. This made a sound of a snorer waking up abruptly. He went to the door, rubbing his eyes.

"Dean Picklodgicer, what brings you here at such an hour?"

"I think you know exactly why I'm here!"

"Chris man, close the door! You're letting in all the bright light," Rich said, shielding his eyes, from the excruciating fluorescence of the hall lights.

"Dean, please explain yourself quickly, my friends really needs their sleep," Chris said, yawning.

"Where were you tonight?"

"Excuse me? I've been right here."

"Were you ever near my office?"

"I might have sleepwalked there; I know my way by heart after all."

"Did you hear anything that happened between a top-level SETI agent and me?"

"Sir, really, I'm tired. I didn't see any—" Chris stopped as he fell asleep right on the SETI agent. The man shook him, and he woke up.

"Fine, I'll leave you alone! Good night!"

"Good afternoon, Dean," Chris said. Chris walked back to his bed, holding the agent's security badge. He had slipped a copy of his student I.D. in the agent's pocket so the guy would never know. He tucked it under his pillow, for later use. He remembered what someone had said earlier that year: "Either we get a high-level security SETI card or . . ." he couldn't remember the rest. But now he had what he needed. The card.

Chris tapped the security camera system to see where the dean had gone. The cameras were inside every hallway, but never

It All Started In Chem Class…

in offices; they were afraid the students might tap it. Chris didn't care, because he would just sneak into offices if the case called for such actions. He watched the dean and the agent go to the agent's shuttle. He observed silently as the dean say something; he couldn't quite make it out. Then, the agent shrugged, spoke quickly to his pilot, and came back to the Café Probe, ironically. There, they talked for what must have been an hour.

Chris took his smallest computer, tapped the systems, and left his room. He couldn't have the others with him. He went to the room with the orb, and searched for a tiny imperfection in the generator, the smallest of cracks, the tiniest sign of meshing gone wrong. He found it. It was maybe half a millimeter, and was simply where two pieces didn't match up quite right. He slid in his new SETI card. The wall flew up in an array of colored keys with strange symbols on it. Chris looked around. Everything was foreign. He recognized a key hear and there, like the infinite symbol of a sideways eight. He checked his computer every thirty seconds to make sure the dean was still preoccupied.

Upon hitting a key, Chris saw a 3-dimensional model of the spaceship they would no doubt be using for the mission the dean was planning. He noticed the capacity was only 150. *What happens to the other 50,* he wondered. He noticed one tile. It was just slightly off. Probably a design flaw. Maybe intentional.

He tapped another key and this time saw a word in large red letters that said: TARGETS: CHRIS JOHNSON, JOHN SMITH, BOB TANKALOVA, RICH FLITHINTEON, AND JORDAN WEENDENAHUE. He noticed other names below theirs, also from their frat, such as Jim, Tricks, and Steve. All that worried him was he was number one on their list. He checked the monitor again. The man just realized he didn't have his card. Chris ran all-out to slip in to his own sweet bed from his roof passage. He slipped into bed right before they knocked. It appeared as though the inspection was over.

CHAPTER 10: THE EXPLANATION

"Excuse me, *Chris!* Are you in there?" The dean seemed very angry.

"Yes, sir. Can I help you?"

"You can return my ID badge *to me for starters!*" Even the agent was screaming.

"Hey, how'd I wind up with this? Look, sir, I'm truly very sorry. I must have fallen asleep and dropped my card. That's what happened. It fell into your pocket. Then, since there were two cards in there, I grabbed yours by mistake. Since I didn't turn on any lights, I didn't know it was yours. Here you go. Ah, thank you for *my* ID badge. Good night, sirs," Chris said. They bought his story.

"Good night, Chris."

"Chris, you stole the guy's ID?" Rich was suddenly wide-awake.

"Yeah," Chris said casually.

"Why?"

"I know why. You went back to the room with that glowing orb, didn't you?" John, too, was awake.

"Yeah. The card worked. I found the model of the ship. Get this: it seats 150 people."

Bob was aroused by the commotion, and spoke up. "But 200 people are going on the mission, right?"

"Exactly. Plus, the ship has one tile off by about a centimeter," he said.

"Can't that blow the whole thing up?" Jordan was the last to wake up.

"Yeah. That's what interested me. Plus, we're the top five on their TARGETS list."

Bob obviously needed to go back to sleep because he said, "Oh boy! That's so cool!" No one should have been sarcastic. Bob went back to sleep, as did everyone else, with thoughts of nothing more than the ship and the computer console.

It All Started In Chem Class...

The next day, there was a meeting for anyone who was either going on the mission, or was an alternate for the shuttle trip. Bob and the rest had been informed they were alternates. So, they went to the Café Probe, where the metting was held. They found the dean—not anyone from SETI—there to greet them.

"Good morning gentlemen. The SETI agent who has been staying with us until the time of departure has taken ill today. I will explain, to the best of my ability, this mission that you will be going on. The purpose is to search for, and hopefully find, extraterrestrial life. The reason that I asked the SETI agency to let us participate is this: I decided that no one would be a better welcoming committee than a group of kids from college. I also felt that a true international college should include those from an alien nation. SETI and also NASA believe that the chances of the existence of life outside our solar system are at least seventy percent. They figure that each sun has an average of seven planets, and seeing as there are at least a few hundred billion stars that we have seen, that's about 28 hundred billion planets. The chance that at least one of those is hospitable is fairly decent. I decided that this project will show *how* you use what you learn here, among other things. The truth is, we will be using a fleet, not the one ship. One ship will have the lab scientists, EEU people, and some others. On several other ships, there will be deep-space design and electronics people. This will be the final exam for everyone majoring in Deep-Space Design. Yes, this is where you will use the ships you have designed. We will also have one extra ship, in case we encounter aliens that have technology less advanced than ours. Does anyone have any questions?"

"Yeah, I do," Bob said. "What happens if we encounter a hostile alien nation?"

"Excellent question. This might seem odd, but we are offering extra credit for any student who wishes to create a second model of weaponry ships, equipped with missiles, laser cannons, and the like. Is anyone interested?"

Chris raised his hand. "Sure, I'll try it. Is there a certain caliber you want? Or is it up to our teachers?"

"Ask the teachers. They know more about these sorts of things than I do. I'm in charge of the mission; they're in charge of providing me with the tools to carry it out. Anything else?"

"What happens if we die?" A nerdy looking kid seemed to have just considered the prospect with the talk of hostile aliens.

"Well, that's a risk I'm willing to take," the dean replied.

"Oh, thanks! I feel much better now," he replied with sincerity and innocence in his voice.

"Well, thank you all for coming. I have arranged with your teachers to assure that you won't be late to class. If there are no other questions, I will leave you now. Thank you again for coming, and I hope to see most of you aboard the shuttle for the last two months of school."

The dean left, smiling. Chris knew it was because the dean thought he had convinced everyone to go. Chris still wasn't so sure. He knew everything wasn't what it appeared to be. But he had finally gotten what he wanted: answers.

CHAPTER 11: THE SPACEBALL STORE

The next day found them sitting luxuriously in their "living room" that was the center of their multiple dormitory. "And we come to yet another boring Wednesday. Homework, watch some HTV, the usual, huh?" John asked his friends.

"Probably," Chris replied. "I don't know about you guys, but I seriously need some new Spaceball stuff. What do ya say?"

"My baton's chipping, my armor's thin, and my board's rusting. Where we gonna get the cash, genius?" Rich answered, irritably.

"Well, everyone put their money on Team DOG to beat us, didn't they? Me, I put 500 on 3D," Chris said, grinning.

"You don't have 500 left!" Jordan exclaimed.

"Exactly. But we won, so I got 100 times what I paid," Chris answered calmly.

"Ah, I see what you mean. Besides, we all had to put in 100 to show support. When are we getting our money?" Rich raised an eyebrow as he talked.

"I stopped by the betting booth on my way out last night. Here you go, and you, and you, don't let me forget you." Chris passed out their shares of money to them. A lot of rich people betted on Team DOG, so they each received lots of money, roughly ten thousand dollars a piece, with an easy fifty for Chris.

"Let's go *shopping!*" John jumped up, money clinched in one hand, as he yelled. First they decided to get some sleep, because it was only 0930 hours SST. Two hours later, they left. They went to the only Spaceball Supply store in existence: Spaceball Supplies and More. It was opened at the same time that Spaceball began. Everyone had to go there to buy their Spaceball supplies, and some people just bought things for fun. They walked in, and began speaking to the man behind the counter. His name was Mike.

"Whoa, little Mike has two jobs now! I'm impressed," John said. It was the same person he met on the shuttle to his class.

"Hey, not everyone can play Spaceball," Mike replied.

"I do believe you mean 'Not everyone is good enough,'" Chris said.

"Yeah, yeah, whatever," Mike said. "Anyway, what do you guys need?"

"Better batons, better boards, better suits. You know, the usual," John answered.

"That really doesn't tell me much. What kind of boards?"

"The best kind. I want a Satellite. What's their newest model called?" Chris favored Satellite brand, for very specific reasons.

"TRI-Angle. Didn't you know that? I mean, dude, they named after . . . Oh, I get it." Mike sighed.

"I suppose I'll take one of those. How have they been selling, anyway?"

"Hottest item. We just got in a new shipment today. They sell so fast, I've memorized the price with tax. And, they also have a new type of attachment. It's called the DDD pad or something like that. It's been selling fairly well. You know anything about it?"

"Yeah, we know. It was named in commemoration of the sophomores, Team DDD. It's supposed to help the steering or something," Rich said.

"Wow, you guys are sure making some cash off of Satellite, huh?"

"Well, we do decently, ya know. We do buy our own products and stuff, so it works out," Jordan replied.

"You mean you still pay for it? Even though it's practically your brand?"

Bob replied, "Sure. They are trying to give out a 'we're not better than anyone else' attitude. Strange, but whatever works for them. I don't really care, because that big fat check is gonna have my name on it. Anyway, what kinds of armor you got now?"

It All Started In Chem Class... 75

"We got your usual green, the red flames, the green flames, and a teddy bear design. Didn't see that in back, oh well. That's about it. What you guys want?"

Chris spoke up, as he was the captain. "I want each of those red flame suits, emblazoned with our number, and a picture of our pets with a blowtorch. And also put the names and numbers on the back."

"Why?"

"I'm thinking we should do a mascot. How about the Flamethrowers?"

"Hey, you're the captain. I don't see why not," Rich said. They went to look at boards while Mike got the space armor ready. It took Mike about an hour to do the artwork.

"This board is nice. Not as good as a Satellite, but I might get one just to cruise around school," John said. "I love how they let us do that, but no one else, ya know?" He was admiring an Anti-Cruz board model Blackdeck. It was a smaller board, just to fly around the school, a way to get from one class to another. Spaceball players were allowed to do this. They got away with a lot of stuff most kids didn't. All of their teachers hated them, as did the Dean. But the dean's boss loved Spaceball, and he liked all the players. So, the dean and teachers had to cut them a lot of slack.

"Whoa, dude, get a look at this beauty," Rich said, eyes wide.

"A new Galaxy Industries! Awesome," Chris said quietly, with admiration.

"No one can make 'em like Galaxy does man. I mean, Satellites are great boards and all, but this is just . . . wow. Perfect balance in such a small package. It's like a dream board come true. No way! It even comes with detachable, reusable Grenade rockets! This has to be the greatest board I've ever seen," John said, a tear in his eye.

"Yeah, and check out the price tag on it," Jordan said. Now John had tears in his eyes for different reasons. It had a price tag bigger than the motor.

"Oh well, moving along, there's also some new sets of Moon Wok. Better designs, too. I like this pair. It has a heating/cooling/massage system in it! These will never wear out! I swear; it even has a lifetime warranty on it! I think I might have to get me a pair of these," Bob said.

"Nah, those aren't me. I'm getting me a pair of Washintens. I like these black and gold colored shoes. Nice grip for a board, too. I could use these for all-around. Chris, when does the check come in?" Rich was eager to spend some money. He still had yet to receive his money from the bets.his money from the Spaceball bets.

"I got some right here for you Rich. How much did you bet?"

"200," Rich said.

"Sure. I got you your 100 worth right here. In fact, everyone come get some money," Chris said, because he didn't want them yelling at him for losing it. He handed out their bet money and their profits from it. They each had a single bill with a number inscribed on it. This was the easiest way to use money, developed in the future. The money was more like a check, except that every store and restaurant accepted it. It worked out really well for them, because they always got bills in different sizes. In the old system, people only had bills that went up to 100 dollars, so you would have to make annoying trips to the bank to get anything smaller. In the future, such annoying trips were eliminated.

"Yeah, I'm getting the Moon Woks. I think I might get this Freeride. Model is called 'Fireball.' It says it has a holographic projection to make it look like you are riding fire itself! Just for cruising, of course," Bob said.

"I have to get my Washintens," Rich said, eyes wide. "I'm also gonna get a backup board, in case my Satellite breaks. Glad I put in that clause in our contract. I think I'll go with a Galaxy Industries. This is a dream to ride, I would imagine."

"Icicle from Anti-Cruz. Nice enough. Ooh, a nice addition, too," Chris said.

Rich asked, "What's that?"

It All Started In Chem Class…

"A twin nitrogen propulsion jet—2Nitro for short. Alternative to an external combustion. I like it. It says it will leave your roommates stone cold. Not much, either." They all paid for what they wanted, and left. They even had some cash left. Chris got two new boards, a backup Galaxy Industries and the Icicle from Anti-Cruz. He also purchased a pair of shoes made by Vacuum. Vacuum shoes had grip so good it was supposed to create a vacuum between the shoes and the board.

In addition to his Washinten shoes, Rich got a Galaxy Industries board. It was a different model than Chris's, though. His was another new one, but designed for power, not speed. It was the type of board that could make average speed with five men trying to stall you. He figured there was no point in getting two of the same, because then you couldn't swap them out—something practiced by most of the Spaceball players. That's why most people on a team tried to have different boards with different purposes. They all waited for their Satellite advertising checks before buying the newest gear from their company.

Mike was done with their suits just in time to ring up their large orders. "Whoa, you guys sure got a lot of stuff. Man, this is enough for two teams!"

"Not really. See, these are hoverboards, while these over here are Spaceboards. Big difference. Anyway, you get the suits done?"

"Actually, I did just a little more." Mike showed them their new suits. They were black with fire along the side, and written across the front "X-tinguishers" in flaming letters. On the back, it had nicknames, instead of their real names, and their numbers. "Rich, how did you get the nickname 'Cashed-Out'?"

"Well, the very first Spaceball match I played in, I had a custom board, a designer suit, and 500 dollar shoes. My parents forced me to do it— it wasn't my idea. So everyone said I had to be cashed out to afford it. The name just sorta stuck. Besides, it's better than Richie Rich. Anyway, thanks for putting on my suit. I like the dollar signs you added," Rich replied.

"Chris, you don't mind the nickname Fireblast, do you?"

"I think it looks pretty cool. Thanks, I've never actually had a nickname in Spaceball before."

"Okay, Bob, I'm not sure why I did this, but I gave you the nickname The Iceman. That won't defeat your flaming image, will it?"

"Not at all. I like the name. Besides, the names don't have to reflect the team concept. So what's Jordan's nickname?"

"Supernova has a nice ring to it, don't you think, Jordan?"

"Sure, sound's great. Thanks Mike." They left and went back to their dorm room on their new hoverboards. Spaceball supplies were the only things they actually enjoyed shopping for.

"Well, it looks like we are going to have another boring week and weekend," Chris said, after they had gone back to the room—stopping by their equipment room to drop off their stuff—and, with their semesters hitting a lull, they drifted off to an early slumber.

CHAPTER 12: THE CHEMISTRY LOUNGE

"Chris, I just got this letter. They 'found' our forms, and we were accepted to go on the mission! It leaves in one week! There's no way out now," John said on Friday morning. Thursday had proven very uneventful, with nothing but tests all day. "We lose."

"Yeah. We'd have to run away to avoid it, and they would still find us. Oh well, let's just go with it. There's no use fighting them now," he said, sighing. "Wait, one week? We have Spaceball finals! How can they schedule it that soon? I don't believe this!"

"Hey, the funny thing is the other team is going with us. At least they can't win by forfeit."

"Hey guys, what's going on?" Rich had awakened up to talk of Spaceball forfeits.

"Rich, we have to go on the mission. They're making us. They forged papers and everything. The dean doesn't give us much choice. But that's the same day as the Spaceball finals. Both teams are going on the mission, so we don't' know what they're going to do about it. But we have to go. You don't mind, do you?"

"Not at all. Did you get the warship done?"

"Yeah, they're making me a dozen of them."

"Construction must be working overtime, then, making you 13 ships," Rich said, yawning.

"Yeah it's pretty cool. I got an 'A' in the class, though. We're using Nitro missiles, laser cannons, and all sorts of stuff. Believe me, we'll have protection. Bob, Jordan," Chris began as he noticed his other friends waking up, "we're going on the mission, dean's orders. He found some papers that we supposedly filled out. We leave in a week. Pack ya bags, men; we're outta here!"

"Yippee," Jordan said in a dry voice. "I suppose it's not *that* bad to be the top five targets of an organization with more secrets than I care to count. Oh well, I gotta go to class. So in a week, construction will be done on your ship?"

"Yeah, the day before we leave. You still have to install the electronics."

"That's cool." Everyone left and went to class, thinking once more of the mission that lay before them.

Chris had no real reason to be in class, so he skipped it. He had a good grade, no matter how you looked at it. Each ship that was built counted as an extra grade for him. He made four designs and three variations on each design. With all the extra grades, he had the highest possible grade. Instead of going to class, he went back to his room and turned on a movie. The only problem would be if a teacher walked by. Then, Chris turned off the movie and decided to sit in on John's class. He had to go in and watch through the air vents, or he would get in trouble. He called John, who wasn't actually in his seat. "Hey, man, I'm in your class," he said.

"Why?"

"I didn't feel like going to mine; it was boring today. So, where are you at?"

"I'm downstairs. There's a special room down here. This station is full of surprises. Where are you at?"

"I'm upstairs, in the vent shafts. How do I get down where you are?"

"Well, there's a secret set of stairs right under the teacher's desk. Wait for him to do a lab experiment, then pop out the screen, put it back, and go down the stairs. You'll see me."

"He's about to ask you a question," Chris whispered hurriedly.

"What's he asking?"

"Mr. Smith, how many kinds of rubber-resistant acids has this class made synthetically?"

"Hang on," John said. He then said something to someone Chris couldn't see, but he saw the hologram speaking the answer to the question.

"Smooth. Mine is asleep in class, but I have it set up with over five hundred answers to anything the teacher asks. Ooh, he's doing another synthetic acid, resilient only to Spaceball armor. Time to make my move," Chris said. He crawled to the ventilation grid right behind the teacher's desk, and slipped out. He replaced the grid, and saw the staircase's rail just sticking out.

"I forgot to tell you, the colors are green, blue, yellow, orange, purple, red." Just as he was about to ask, Chris saw what he meant. There was a key panel with those colors on it. He punched them in the order John told him. Suddenly, the floor slid back to reveal a staircase leading downstairs to what could only be the cargo bay.

"Alright, that was easy enough. Now, please turn to page 541 in your chemistry book, and do the work on that chapter while I grade your tests," the teacher said.

"John, how do I get the floor closed?"

"Just run down here as fast as you can. Why?"

"Experiment was really fast. He's on his way back down." Chris ran as fast as he could. The floor panel closed just as he heard the teacher sit down. Chris entered into a billiard room with a lighted wall, a large boom box, and John.

"Hey, glad you could make it! I can't believe it took me more than half a year to find this place! This thing is soundproof! I'd seen him go places from the air vent, but I never knew where! Sometimes, he has the isolation booths that come down. I realized that's when he does it. He gets down here, cranks up the music, has himself some food; Teachers are lucky! By the way, did you say he was going to grade papers?"

"Yeah, why?"

"He's coming down here! There's only one way to get out without him seeing us. One of the ceiling tiles is a false tile that will go right to my desk. He had it installed to find out if I was using a decoy in class. It's how I still get out when he comes down. Come on!" They raced to the panel, and hit it. It slid out, revealing a tunnel to John's desk. They crawled out to find the isolation booth in place, and John's hologram in working hard mode. Then Chris realized the problem with the isolation chambers. There was only one way out and that was down. They either had to go down into the lounge, or wait until the chamber was raised, revealing them both there. Chris went halfway down the tunnel and watched the teacher. Then, he saw something he had overlooked when he was down there: the bathroom. The teacher went into a door clearly marked "RESTROOM."

"John, he's in the bathroom! How do I go back up the staircase and get out?"

"I don't know! Try hitting the little green button!"

"Okay, thanks!" Chris slid down the tunnel and sprinted to the stairs. He dashed up, trying to make as little noise as possible. He saw the little green button and pressed it. The ceiling slid up just as the teacher came out. Chris ran up, closed the floor, and went in the air vent shafts. Fortunately for him, class was almost over. The teacher stayed in the lounge for another half hour before coming out.

"Class dismissed!" Chris found John once the shuttle had docked in the station.

"Nice job on the escape," John commented as they hovered back to the Café Probe for lunch.

"Thanks. That place is cool! We might have to go back sometime," Chris replied.

CHAPTER 13: THE CAFÉ PROBE SECRET

"I bet that's not the only teacher lounge here," John said, grinning. "I mean, this place has hundreds of secrets. Of course, we *do* know about half of them. I mean, have you ever wondered where the faculty meetings are held? It has to be somewhere the students don't know about, or else we would know all their secrets. And so far, we haven't seen any teacher meetings, have we?"

"Good point. I bet there is at least one fake floor tile here. Hey, there's Bob, Jordan, and Rich. They didn't bring their boards. I bet a teacher took them away. Let's go eat lunch," Chris said. John made him look for oddities in the floor tiles. One little thing off could give him all he needed. The ceiling tiles were metallic, to protect against meteor showers and events similar to that. This also made it easier to clean the floors off. There weren't very many tiles, so cracks in the floors were rare. This was one way Chris would notice a secret exit, assuming there was one.

"Hey guys. Where've you been at?" Rich greeted Chris and John.

"Some secret lounge under John's classroom," Chris said nonchalantly.

"Cool," Bob said, "I guess you'll have to take us down there sometime."

"Yeah. John thinks the probe has a secret room, like the Chem shuttle."

"I never said it *did*; I said it *might*," John said indignantly. "You never know until you find out!" As he said that, Chris noticed a stain in the steel. They had gotten sidetracked, and walked off away from the tables.

"Hey, check that out! There's a stain in the stainless steel!"

"That's interesting. That would also be hard to do. I mean, they don't call it stainless for no reason," Rich said. "Kick it with your shoe."

"After you," Bob said. Rich kicked it, and nothing happened.

"I've got an idea," Chris said. There was quiet applause. "Seriously. What if they designed this so that only teachers could go down there? What if you need a retina scan and stuff like that?"

"Fine," Rich said, "try it out." Chris touched his thumb to it. Apparently, the pressure of his thumb was enough. A small area of the floor slid back. Now, his entire arm would fit in. He reached in and found a control console. He typed randomly, trying to use different combinations of keys, hoping something might work.

"Chris, use this," John said. He handed Chris a small device used only to crack codes. Within seconds, a spiral staircase appeared. Rich led the way down. Below, they found something that wasn't even close to what they had expected.

"Whoa! It's the security room! I've been looking for this place all year," Bob said in awe.

"Yeah, but there's bound to be someone in here. They wouldn't just walk off and leave it, would they?" Chris shrugged. Then he noticed someone in there. He closed the panel with the same code cracker, and they all left to eat lunch. Chris had managed, however, to slip a digitally recording camera the size of a dime onto the ceiling of the security room. He planned to look at the room later. He didn't really want to use it to cheat off tests or anything; it was simply a way for him to pass the time. Many of his pastime activities did usually get him a trip to the dean's office.

They took their time eating lunch. Only Rich had an afternoon class, and he was willing to miss it. No one really liked history, and lectures were the worst part. Rich only went to lectures if he knew he was going to be tested over the material. Otherwise, he would just copy someone else's notes. Rich could for the most just read ahead in his holobook. Rich liked his holobook because he could read it while walking down the hall, but because of its slight transparency, he could still watch where he was going. And it was also helpful to have his magic pen, which would send out light signals and tell the holobook what sections to highlight, underline, or make special marks by. It really helped him study. As he was reading his holobook, he noticed everyone

It All Started In Chem Class...   85

else leaving, staring at him, thinking he was about to have a test. A lot of people did that kind of studying, but not Rich.

"They are," Chris said, waiting for the last person to leave, "gone!" With that last word, they got up and went to the spot where the steel was stained. The spot was gone. They checked in several different places; they searched everywhere, but to no avail. The spot had disappeared all together. It was nowhere to be found. But, Chris would not give up. He looked all around the spot, looking for his thumb mark, finally coming across it. He saw this thumb mark because it made the steel look blemished, just barely. He pushed on it, but nothing happened. He couldn't figure it out.

"It moved," John said. Everyone looked curiously at him, so he continued. "Whatever it was is on a track. The keypad we used to open the staircase. It runs on a track, so it's only in the same place for a minute or two. It's somewhere else in here. I guess we should just forget about it." He looked around, looking for nonexistent signs of approval on his friends' faces.

"No way. I doubt that's just a security room. There's probably a whole lot more down there," Chris said. "Besides, my video camera is still recording." He smiled upon seeing their looks of shock and amaze.

Rich was struck with a sudden idea. "What if we just go through the kitchen?"

"Sounds like fun," John answered. The five roommates went to the kitchen, and looked for something else out of the ordinary. John kept the cooks busy by asking about renewing his meal card without having any good money. He made them mad but it worked.

Rich still wasn't sure what he was doing there. He wasn't really reluctant or anything; he just didn't figure out what was so good about finding a security room. But, he did want to get Chris's camera. He looked around for something weird, but he knew the thing out-of-place could be as subtle as a higher ledge that could make you trip. He thought about this option as he hit his toe on a slightly raised portion of the room. He called Chris on his holophone, so that the cooks wouldn't hear them talking. "Yeah, I found this section of tiles that's raised. About a three centimeters from the other section. You should come look at," he told Chris.

Chris walked over to Rich, looking for some entrance to below. He saw what Rich meant. He bent down to look at the tiles more closely. In the kitchen, they had ceramic tiles, because it gave the cooks more traction to prevent them from slipping and breaking their back with grease all over them. He had to think of how to open the secret entrance.

John continued to aggravate the head cook, asking about the food, the drinks, and various other things until Chris called him. "Hey, what's up? Okay. Why? Oh. Are you sure? Well that's comforting," he said. He walked over to where Chris was.

"John," Chris said over his holophone. "We need you over here. We think it takes at least three or four people to trigger this. Not really. Whatever. Just get over here!" John saw what they were looking at. It was apparently an elevator of some sort. It looked more traditional than the single-person pods they were accustomed to. John saw Bob, Rich, Chris and Jordan were already there, stomping on it. It wasn't working for them, so John got on. It still didn't work, so John used his last option. He called the animals on their holophones, and told them to come to the kitchen. They obeyed, and soon they had the entire dorm room standing there. Someone else kept the cooks busy. It was the dean, coincidentally. He was inadvertently helping them. As he talked, John felt the ground shake. It wavered and wobbled, probably trying to scare off anyone who didn't know what they were doing. At least, John hoped it was that simple. Everyone else was lowered into a room where there was a computer display. It asked for valid teacher identification.

Chris used his sternest voice and said, "Come on, don't give me that! You know exactly who I am. Look, Dean Picklodgicer is in the process of getting me a new I.D. made. You and I both know about that acne outbreak, don't we?"

"Very well," the computer said, "Proceed to the teacher check-in and get your complementary raffle tickets. Keep in mind that today's prize is a space scooter!"

It All Started In Chem Class...

"Yeah right," Chris said out loud. He and his friends walked right past the raffle ticket table, grabbing a few tickets each. The lady handing them out just looked bewilderedly at them. Then she shrugged and turned back. The air about Bob just seemed to make him seem important. No one seemed to notice them, probably because they had on suits and glasses. Chris had brought some with him, just in case it called for it. He kept them in a certain briefcase, and he brought it when he snuck onto John's shuttle. As they walked, they saw soda machines with huge discounts, big screen televisions, and satellite dishes. They stayed down there for a full hour.

"Hey, check out this movie! It's some really old Stars Wars flick. Two dimensions. Look at those horrible graphics! I mean, those are just pitiful," Chris commented. They played some people, watched HTV, maxed out on sodas, and went back to their dorm rooms. Then Chris remembered his camera. John offered to go back and get it.

"Sure, man, I don't mind at all!" John went back to the room, using the same method and using weights. Once he was down, he walked around and asked for directions to the security room. His history teacher was happy to tell him how to get there.

"What is your security entry level and password?" The man inside the room was just following protocol. John had to get him to break it.

"Password? Sir, they don't issue passwords to those of us with level six clearance codes," he said coolly.

"Really? Level six?"

"Ty," John finished. "Level sixty."

"Right. Actually, there *is* no level sixty," the security officer replied.

"Oh, oh my goodness! Thank God you're okay! Oh you poor soul I've been looking all over this whole college for you! Officer, this man hit his head on a very low ledge; it knocked him out. He's been hallucinating about being an incredibly intelligent CIA officer. I'm so very sorry for the interruption," Chris said. While the officer was trying to figure out what was going on and how to respond, Chris took John and led him swiftly into the heart of the security room.

He looked for his security camera. He saw the officer coming behind him. "John, act delusional, man," Chris whispered. Then, he spotted the camera. It must have moved three and a half, maybe four, meters, he guessed. John began to ask people if they knew what happened to the secret codes. Chris left him, and went to the camera. John saw him, and didn't care. That's why they were down there. Chris couldn't reach the camera. They had tall ceilings in the security and surveillance room. Chris needed some stilts. Then he remembered his Icicle. But if he used it, the teachers would know who he was. He heard a familiar noise. Comet, his tiger, had somehow sneaked into his coat pocket while he wasn't looking. He noticed that Comet didn't have on his Spaceball uniform. *Great,* he thought, *I'll have to throw him.* Then, John came over.

"They're calling the dean. We can get out right up there. I checked with the other teachers; they've had to use it a lot before. Did you get the camera?"

"Not yet. I'm about to." Then to Comet, he said, "Okay, buddy, go get the camera." He threw Comet up, and Comet somehow landed on the ceiling. He grabbed the camera, and jumped back down. This caused total pandemonium in the security room. Chris took Comet and ran to the exit John had pointed to, with John right behind him. They got out, but just barely. They knew the security guards would come after them, so they took off their teacher clothes and glasses, to reveal street clothes. They packed the costumes, and hopped on their hoverboards. Chris checked with John to make sure he was ready, and they took off. They were in the safety of their own dorm rooms by the time the dean got to the scene of the incident.

"Well, that was certainly fun. Another secret discovered; another mystery explored. I'm done for now," John said.

"Yeah, good idea," Chris answered. They were both exhausted. But John was right. The school had two less secrets now. And Chris had twelve hours of live feed from that room.

CHAPTER 14: THE FINAL ASSIGNMENT

"The countdown to the end begins. Day six."

"John it's only 0930 man! Go back to sleep," Rich said as he threw a pillow at him. It was Saturday, and they all wanted to sleep in. Everyone, apparently, except for John, who was wide awake.

"I can't sleep, knowing it's only six days away," he said nervously.

"Would you please shut up?" Rich picked his pillow and hit John over the head once again. He had hoped it would knock him unconscious, but he had no such luck. John realized no one cared, and went back to sleep.

A few hours later, they all got up. John was still worrying about the mission. Jordan was somewhat concerned with his grade, while Chris was thinking about designing a cruiser. He wondered if SETI had realized they would need a deep-space cruiser. This would provide an excellent scout ship for the mission. He felt a scout ship would be one of the biggest components in the fleet.

"Chris, do we have practice today?" Bob wasn't really in the mood for practice, especially since they would miss their very last game. Bob loved the sport, just not practicing for a game that in all likelihood would never take place.

"Yep. We have a few new things to go over. Pretty simple, except for the twin helix," he answered.

"Ooh, what's that? Is it a double helix?"

"Sort of. It's two double helixes running parallel. It seemed sort of easy when the coach told me about it, but I think it might take just a little bit of work. You guys up to it?"

"Yeah," they replied in unison. They all got dressed into their Spaceball equipment, and sat down to watch the HTV. They didn't have much longer before practice started.

"Okay," Chris said. "I'm ordering pizza for lunch before we go." They all nodded. After they ate, they went to practice, all riding their hoverboards.

"Good afternoon, gentlemen," the coach said. "I hope you all slept well. I see you have new equipment. Very nice. Anyway, I heard you were elected to go on that mission. I will miss coaching you in the finals, but that's the way the ball bounces, I suppose. Best of luck to all of you.

"But now the important thing, just in case you play another game before you leave, is the Twin Helix. Chris and John, you get one helix. Rich and Jordan, you get another. Bob, your job is fly straight between them. Everyone will think you have the Spaceball, but you won't. See, Rich and Jordan will have it. They will volley it at the cross of the double helix, and then, halfway down, they will hit it to you, Bob, and you will carry it and create a triple helix with Chris and John. This will eventually merge into Rich and Jordan's double helix, creating a five-man helix. We will have three men flying parallel, those being John Chris and Bob, in total contradiction to Rich and Jordan, who will be flying the other way. A twin helix has been done, but the fifth man is the wild card. That is what throws off the balance of the maneuver. It also makes it nearly impossible to counter. The animals will just ride with you on it. Sound easy?"

"Not at all," Chris said.

"Clear as quantum physics," Rich said.

"Oh well, you aren't the coach! I am, which gives me the total power of this group," he said with a grin.

"Not if I do this," Chris said, as he pretended to hit him with his baton, stopping millimeters from his coach's face.

"Anyway, get started," Coach Beale said. They ran the twin helix, which was simple enough for the experienced team. Bob had the most difficult part, merging into a double helix already in motion. They ran fine, up until the halfway point. They practiced the merging over and over. Then, they got the three-man helix going. Chris liked doing hard moves, because it really took his mind off the other problems of life. It took his mind off

It All Started In Chem Class…

problems like ships and missions and SETI. This was because as soon as he thought about things like that, he messed up badly on his maneuvers. Then, he had to do it again. By the end of the day, they were doing it almost perfectly.

"Well, I don't want to work you guys too hard. Get back to the dorm, and do, uh, whatever it is you do there. See you later!" They all put their boards on slow, and Bob put his shoes on the massage therapy setting. It took them longer, but they all enjoyed the ride back to the dorm rooms.

"Hey, when are you guys gonna pack?"

"Well, John, I plan to wait until an hour before to pack my bags," Rich replied with sarcasm.

"I'm not planning on it now, but we do need to get ready," John said aggravated.

"Whatever. Right now, I'm gonna do a little bit of homework, then watch some good old HTV," Chris said.

"I thought your grade was already flawless," Jordan said.

"Well, I still need all the skills for the mission, ya know," he answered quickly. He got out his holobooks, and opened to the pages he had digitally bookmarked in each. He had a few chapters left that he was supposed to read by the end of the year. Everything he read he would be tested on, during the SETI mission.

"Yeah, I need to catch up, too. The teach wants me to take the final exam before I leave. Plus, I have to build a complete matter teleportation unit. Oh yeah, I told you about that one. Anyway, I'm only halfway done. I wish those stupid idiots had forged those papers earlier! Oh well, I'll be in my section of the room," Rich commented. They all went to their rooms, each with their own assignment to complete. After practice, they had little free time, with the exception of eating dinner. Before and after that, they never came out of their rooms.

"FINALLY! All my homework for the whole year is done," Chris exclaimed happily. "That's the one great thing about this college. You know most of your homework from day one, and you can do it as you please at your own pace," he commented.

"Yeah, whatever. I like it because my mom and dad can't drive down to check on me," Bob replied. They had all finished their final projects and were sitting around watching a movie in HTV. They had a full week of college left, but they felt light and happy. Of course, that feeling of dread did always linger in the back of their minds.

"Ah, I've seen this a dozen times. I'm gonna go ride my Icicle around for a while. See if I can find someone to show it off to," Chris told the rest of the group.

"Hey, I bet you fifty I can beat it with my Fireball," Bob stated.

"Fine, let's go," Chris responded.

"You wanna choose the spot, or should I?"

"The underspace, I suppose," Chris answered thoughtfully. "They haven't found that place yet, have they?"

"Not that I know of," Rich said. The underspace was a large shelter under the main part of the ship. It wasn't really underground, so they called it underspace. It was the only secret kids had from teachers. Someone had slipped the construction workers a large sum of money to add it and tell the teachers it was part of a reentry fuel cell. The teachers bought it, and the students had a large underground arena for unauthorized activities, such as space races.

Chapter 15: A Day at the Races

With those reassuring words from Rich, they left for the underground, suits on and boards in hand. When they got there, they saw the team they should have been facing in the finals was already there.

"Well well well. The almighty has arrived," the captain for their should-be opposition said. "We don't see your kind around here much," he sneered.

"My kind?"

"Yeah, you know, goody goody types. I mean, we come down here all the time. First time I've seen you here in, well, ever! I guess you were all off practicing."

"No, we were off making money to buy these boards. And for your information, we only practice once a week. And also, how much did it cost to make the finals?"

"Cost? You think we had to *pay* to make the finals? Come on, not *everyone* is that pathetic!"

"Well, I was just thinking that some people make it by skill, and others, well—"

"We're not quite sure how some people made the finals," Bob finished.

"You want to see some skill? Okay then! I'll show you some! Let's go, right here, right now. I put my custom Pacificruz against whatever you call that piece of junk," the captain, Will, replied.

"Fine. How much you want to bet?"

"How much you got?"

"More than you," Bob said, drawing his wallet. It was full of large bills. Will pulled out a wallet with the same amount of money, roughly. They handed them to someone who didn't take sides, known simply as Ref. Ref took the wallets, and counted the money.

"Lots of cash riding on this race, gentlemen," Ref said. "Anyone want to put money on it?" A lot of kids that were waiting for a race ran up with money in their hands. A lot of people worked in various places aboard the station, at restaurants and other places of interest aboard the station and used their money to make bets.

"Alright," Ref said, "It's time to do this. I will fly out into the middle of the track, and throw down this towel, signaling the start of the race. We have three people at the end to see who breaks the tape first. The first person to break the tape, once agreed upon by the three judges, will be the undisputed winner. First rule is there are no rules! Are there any questions?" After a pause, he continued. "Best of luck to both of you. Please, don't break bones; I hate to clean up the blood. Well, as long as everyone is clear on what we're doing, let's get started!"

With a loud round of applause and shouting, they turned on their engines. Bob's board turned fiery red when he started up. Everyone whooped and hollered. Will turned on his, and it turned jet-black. This wasn't quite as impressive, but they clapped. Then, the air seemed to grow thick with tension as Ref raised his hand for silence.

He threw it down, and they had blown past him before it hit the ground. The boards were evenly matched. As they flew, they were neck and neck. No one knew what was going to happen. The distance they had to race was the length of at least fifty football fields, and they were easily traveling 1 MAU, which was 93 miles an hour. This was one of the only times that miles per hour were still used, solely because of the simplicity of the conversion. MAU meant Micro Astronomical Unit, which represented one millionth of an astronomical unit.

They raced, neck and neck, Bob gaining a centimeter, Will then gaining as much. Chris was betting money— a lot of money—on Bob's winning. He noticed that Will was going to the left, just barely. Bob noticed too. He fishtailed, and knocked Will's ankles out. Will was caught off-guard. He didn't expect the "goody-goody" to do something flat-out wrong like that. Of course, nothing in illegal racing was actually "right" but what Will thought about, and also what Bob did, was bad sportsmanship.

It All Started In Chem Class…

This move by Bob put him far ahead, but just made Will more determined to win.

Will slowed down briefly, but was soon racing even faster than before. With his custom board, he had special systems to give him jets of speed, like miniature rockets attached to the back of his board. He had planned on using them for the home stretch, but he used them sooner, throwing his entire plan askew. He was only about a meter behind his opponent now, Bob noticed angrily in his rear-view glasses. He began to swerve in and out, testing Will's agility. Will did the exact opposite of what Bob was doing; when Bob went in, he went out, continuing for about ten seconds.

They lined up for the home stretch. Bob had one motor he hadn't used yet. Will had six rockets. They leaned down, strapped on their shoes, and applied the last bit of fuel. They both knew how much was riding on the race. Chris waited to see when John would kick in the last motor at full. It was running half, because he didn't want to burn it out. He saw Will slowly burning his rockets.

Then, in an instant, Will ignited all of his rockets at one time, sending him flying ahead. John kicked in the last motor to full, and applied all the auxiliary force he had. He caught up to Will as they were about ten meters away from the finish line. The judges watched in anticipation. They all had to look straight ahead so that they didn't see someone come across at an angle, or with obstructed vision. They were racing neck and neck, about to cross. No one knew who would be first, not even Will or Bob. Will threw something at Bob's board, but Bob deflected it right back at Will. Whatever Will had thrown backfired, and his board stalled at the very edge of the red ribbon they were required to break. Bob cut his motors to half power as he crossed the line, in a mockingly slow fashion, waving to all those on his side of the track.

"We have a winner!" Ref took Bob's hand and thrust it into the air. He handed him the prize money, and the money he bet on the race. It was a large sum of money.

Chris was next. He was psyched for his race. He was racing a sophomore from the team known as DOG. His name was

Clarence. "Clarence, huh? Boy, I feel sorry for anyone that has to name their own kid Clarence. Did they smack you across the head at birth?"

"No," Clarence replied shortly. He was a large man of African descent. He had a Cruzzer board called OceanBlue. This was because of its blue appearance and its soft waterbed for his feet to rest on. It was equal to Chris's board in price and most likely power. Chris knew it would be a good race. He watched as a layer of water spread over the board.

Ref didn't even bother to repeat the instructions. He just flew out to the middle, and raised his hands. The room was silent almost instantly. Chris and Clarence both turned their engines to rest. It would keep them from moving until they hit it into full throttle. He threw down the towel, and they took off!

Chris had two nitrogen motors for propulsion. They were both positioned centrally, to allow him to use one if he wanted to. He was only using one to let Clarence over-estimate his own speed, while not realizing the Icicle's full potential. Chris had a reputation for pulling stuff more so than Bob. He had to let Clarence get a fair distance ahead, as the first part of his plan. In hoverboard racing, it wasn't the type of race where racers hit it all-out from the start of the race. They took it half power sometimes, and full power others. It all depended on the situation, the length, the opponent, and the board.

Clarence had about five meters on Chris when things started to change. Chris kicked his motors all the way. He turned them both to full, soaring ahead. This truly surprised Clarence, who was almost knocked off his hoverboard. Clarence had just realized the true potential of Chris's board. Within seconds, Chris was racing alongside Clarence. Clarence spun out, hitting Chris in the ankles, and knocking his board off-course. Chris tried to correct, but Clarence was blocking his way. So, he did the only thing he could—he moved to the left wall of the race, and sped up, using every bit of his auxiliary power.

Chris and Clarence entered the home stretch, both using all they had. Chris still had one trick up his sleeve. One reason he bought the board was because of the icy path it left. Clarence hit him already, so he did something just as bad in retaliation. He threw it into hyperdrive, which would only last for a few seconds. It was just enough to put him ahead of Clarence. He swerved back in front of Clarence, and slowed down, just barely.

Clarence felt the icy jets of Chris's board on him. They were freezing him, numbing his toes. He realized that this was Chris's plan from the very beginning. *Good job,* he thought. He watched as the freezing power crept up his legs, icing his entire body. This made steering his board next to impossible. *At least it hasn't gotten my motor yet,* he thought. He hoped Chris had some humanity left in him.

Chris moved into the lane where Clarence started. He had done his damage. He knew Clarence couldn't go as fast with only mobility from the waist up. He didn't want to kill him, just win the race. And it appeared, as he went the last few meters maintaining a fair lead, as though he had done it. He was almost out of his auxiliary power, though. He wouldn't have enough to get him through the end. He swerved back in front of Clarence, and hit the afterburners, sending him once again into hyperdrive. This lasted just long enough for him to win, Clarence right behind him. He collected his winnings and waved to his fans. With a win each, Chris and John left. It was a great night, and they both left with twice what they came with. The best part was that they weren't found out by the administration..

CHAPTER 16: THE TRAINING

"Day four." It was Monday. Everyone had woken early for their classes. Monday meant early classes, all morning. Even though everyone was up, they weren't really ready yet.

"*John, for the last time,*" Rich said as he body slammed John back into his own bed. John had been trying to wake Rich up in a very unruly manner, which called for his friend, who was—unbeknownst to John—was already awake. Then he got up, dusted himself off, and went to the floating couch where his stuff was. Then, he realized that his project hadn't been tested. "Sorry about that John. Here, try this on. It will ease the pain," he said, grinning evilly. He tossed John his mobile matter teleportation unit. He had a quarter sitting in the other port. A matter teleportation unit has two ports, one where an object is placed and one where the object is sent. "You have to walk around a little bit, though," he told John. John did as he was told, thinking it would help to numb the pain. Rich hit the button, and saw the quarter appear on John's back. John turned around to see it fall into his hand.

"Rich, what's this all about?"

"Yes! It works! Sorry about that one, John. That is my mobile targeting matter teleportation unit. I tested it on you, and it worked."

"Great, I'm so glad *I* got to be the test dummy!" John took it off and threw it back to Rich. "Oh well, I gotta get to class," he said, resigned, walking out the door with his shoulders hung low.

"Not today," Jordan said. "I just got this via C-Mail. We have training today through Friday." C-Mail was college mail, sent straight to holocomps, which were like computers, only, like everything else created in the future, holographic. Holochips, which allowed things to be projected in the third dimension, revolutionized electronics of the future.

"Training?"

It All Started In Chem Class...

"Yeah, for the mission. Letter reads like this: 'To whom it may concern: Congratulations on being selected for the mission. As you know, we will leave this Friday. Many of the things you might encounter along the way haven't been covered in your textbooks. Therefore, we are offering—requiring rather—a five-day training session to prepare for this mission. You must complete all of your assignments outside of class, and have them turned in before you leave. Those of you who don't do this will be replaced. All alternates are required to attend training. It will begin every day at 1000 hours, SST. I will see you there! Signed, the dean.'"

"Woohoo! No more classes for the rest of the year!"

"Yeah," Chris said. "Instead we get training. So much fun." The sarcastic tone in his half-open eyes was apparent.

"Well," John said, "at least I don't have to leave for another two hours." They all left anyway, to eat breakfast. They entered the Café Probe, walking with their hoverboards. They didn't want to use their motors; they might need them for training. They all ate food from the buffet table, which served regular Earth foods. Chris loved the fact that nutrient-packed pills were only a misconception of futuristic eating. Nothing could ever replace the taste of fresh grits in his mouth. They ate very well, because they didn't know how long training lasted, how many breaks they would be allotted, assuming there would be some.

"Everyone who has that special training, you need to leave now! The training will take place on the training module shuttle. Please report now," the automated intercom voice said. Rich knew about how to get there, but he didn't feel like walking. He had already made a large deporting port for the teleportation unit. He took the receiving port, and threw it like a discus. It landed on the shuttle, near the ship bay. Rich stepped into the MTU port, and motioned for his friends to do the same. When they were on the pad, he hit the button, and they teleported to the shuttle..

John felt like his head was on spin cycle. Of course, he also realized how many different pieces his head was in. The way that matter teleportation worked was fairly simple to understand.

Everyone, or everything, was broken down to the smallest parts, and then channeled, and reconstructed at the opposite end. It was actually a simple concept, just one difficult to put into action.

They arrived on board the shuttle to find what one might expect: several desks, some chairs, and a complete submersion room, where they would probably do the majority of the training. That room would make them feel as though they were in space. It was rigged with holographic projections, and hydraulic motion pads to give them the intensity of hitting a meteor. They saw several characteristic SETI agents in black suits. Chris saw the dean off to one side.

"Good morning, gentlemen! I hope you are ready for a full day of training," the dean said cheerfully. *Oh great,* Chris thought. *We're done for now; the dean's happy to see us and we're not in trouble.*

"Sure!" Rich tried to sound truthful, and did a horrible job of it. He sounded so fake that it wasn't even funny. They walked in and dropped their stuff on the back row of desks. Then they approached the dean.

"So, what are we gonna be doing?" John took out his digital holoplanner to make himself a schedule.

"Well, first we are going to get you guys inside a special simulation shuttle. You're going to have to practice making on-the-spot solutions and things. Your particular department will most likely be developing acidic solutions that will respond to things like asteroids and meteors, but not glass. This makes it easier for us to maneuver in the asteroid belt. Chris and Jordan, you will be the pilots of the leading ship, the scout ship, if you prefer. You will both be in an environment with the controls identical to the ship *you* designed. If you can't work it, you will feel intense pressure from the hydraulic systems. Keep in mind; they are on *all* sides of the module shuttle. Rich, do you have the mobile teleportation unit ready?"

"Yes, sir," Rich answered as he pulled it out from underneath his desk.

It All Started In Chem Class...

"Excellent. We are going to scan that for use in the sim. Bob, you know exactly what your job is, right?"

"If we encounter anything unusual, I have to take a reading on it. If it seems to be alive or radioactive, I take it in an airtight sample jar, correct?"

"Very good. Well, John, you may go ahead and begin. The rest of the group will have to train as soon as they get here," the dean said. John entered the submersion room by himself. Slowly, more people trickled in. The dean waited until the class was full to repeat the instructions he had given to Chris and his friends. All of the acidic specialists entered the room with John.

John was amazed at the technology. Just as the dean said, it appeared as though John were on the very ship they were going to take. Seeing a lab station with his name on it, John walked over and examined the ingredients he had to work with. It wasn't quite as good as his dorm lab, but it was decent for basic acids. It had sulfur, which was key in acid making, and a lot of other things that he liked to use as well. He turned around and saw the dean at the front. Then the ship left, and other than a slight shaking sensation, it was a smooth "take-off". Within minutes, they were flying past the moons of Mars, and soon even Mars itself. It all looked so real! Then John heard several other people specializing in his area come in. They went to their lab stations beside his, and got to work. "Whoa, wait a second; what are we supposed to be doing?"

"Making something that will melt ice, and dissolve rock, but is sensitive to glass and steel. Didn't the dean tell you?" John wasn't surprised to hear a nerd answer.

"He said something like that, but he ended with 'things like that,'" Bob started working, however, on the acidic missiles they were supposed to be preparing.

"Wait, I don't get it," some junior Bob had seen in Spaceball said. "Why did we develop a dozen warships if we have to make acidic missiles?"

"I don't know. Besides, this is just a sim, not the real thing," Bob said, using the slang term for simulator.

"Yeah, I guess you're right," the student, named Mike, answered. "Oh shoot! We're almost in the asteroid belt!"

"Here, I'm done," John said quickly.

"Okay," the senior who had assumed command said. "Make me another few liters of it. Give those four the recipe," he replied shortly. John was rushed to make some more of the acid, but he did as the senior said. In his division, there were four seniors, two juniors, two sophomores, and him. He gave the recipe to the juniors and sophomores the senior had mentioned. They all began working on it, while the seniors were hard at work constructing glass containers for them to go in. Glass would work best because it would shatter on impact, and neither the glass nor the acid would harm the actual ship. Making glass, and also forging it into missile-like shapes, was a fairly long process. The ship, which was built for a large number of people, had little maneuverability, so it had to compensate with the acid missiles.

"Can't we just send it out in test tubes?" John watched as a large asteroid loomed. Just because it was a simulation didn't mean he couldn't be knocked flat on his back.

"I suppose we can do that until we get some more glass cans made," Mohammed said. Mohammed, who was from Saudi Arabia, was the senior in charge. With those words, John and the other four lower classmen loaded the test tubes into the launching bay. He was put in charge of aiming them at the asteroids that posed a threat. He fired, hit one direct center, and watched as it split into several smaller asteroids. He had defended them from one, so far. Then he fired three more, getting two direct hits and one near miss. All of the larger asteroids that were in the ship's way were gone. He felt the ground shake slightly as the fragments hit.

"Excellent work," the dean said as he entered the shuttle. "You are through for the day. Tomorrow you will work on developing acids that go through moons and nothing else. This will help us discover more about the cores of the satellites of our solar system. But, all in all, it will be much of the same. I doubt that you will have any problem. Now, please leave so that the next scheduled session may begin." They left, as Chris, Jordan, and other people similarly majoring entered.

"Gentlemen, for this simulation, you will each share a separate booth with one other person. We have you divided based upon majors. One student who designs a ship, and another who works with electronics will occupy one booth. The simulation has the ship that each of you constructed programmed into the booth with your name on it. Have fun, and keep in mind that sims can be deadly. Be careful, and do not goof off. This could cost you your life, as well as the life of the man beside you. I will be back later to see how each of you have progressed," the dean said.

Chris and Jordan walked over to what looked like a cubicle, and sat down in chairs labeled with their names. "They're about to turn on the sim," Chris said.

"Yeah, I know. Don't worry about me. I know how to work this thing. Besides, we're gonna be in training for five days, anyway," Jordan said. Suddenly, he felt the ceiling curve into the aerodynamic body of a deep-space cruiser. He saw the control console that he had created appear in front of him. And he saw the windshield, looking out into space. "Wow, I never would have expected how real this is," he commented, awestruck.

"Yeah, and we haven't even hit an asteroid yet," Chris said. "All right, time to go! Jordan, show me how to steer and stuff, and I'll do what I can."

"Okay, watch carefully. This lever determines the speed. You pull it down to change the speed of the machine, okay? Now, these two joysticks are steering. Concept of them is really simple. First, let me get it going here," Jordan instructed Chris as he turned it to a level three speed. "Now, this controls the height of the ship. Move it forwards and you go down; move it backward and you go up. Now, once you are at a nice cruising altitude, like we are now, this other joystick is for steering. It's easy to use. Move it forward, like I'm doing, to move forward. To turn, move the joystick to that side, like this. If you just lean it to one side, you will initiate side thrusters, which will cause you to move laterally. Move it backward, and you move backward. In case there's someone behind us, I'm not going to try this. Now you try it. Just move us through the asteroid belt or maybe past Jupiter," Jordan continued.

"Okay, this is a piece of cake! I mean, I thought you would whip out all kinds of weird stuff that made my head spin, but you didn't. I'm impressed!" Chris exclaimed. He moved the joysticks around, and even pulled a couple of tricks. "Fasten your seatbelt; we're going upside down!" Once they were in space, they weren't really weightless unless they had the gravitation device off, and they weren't accelerating. When Chris took it upside down, they were accelerating, so they still had some semblance of gravity aboard the simulation. It felt so incredibly real that Jordan had to hang on to his armrest to stop from falling on the ceiling. "I told you to fasten your seatbelt! You ought to listen to me more," Chris said grinning.

"Listen, we're supposed to go to the edge of the solar system and turn back. We're also supposed to report anything unusual," he told Chris.

"Fine, let's do all the things that *you* wanna do!" Chris did it anyway. He flew around Mars and through the asteroid belt. "Hey man, we're behind! I'm gonna crank up the speed," he said as he turned the speed up to five, the second highest speed setting. "We are supposed to the scout ship, after all."

"Okay, that's fine with me. In fact, you're the engineer; you can take it the whole trip," Jordan said, yawning. "I'm gonna go to sleep. Wake me up when the sim is over."

"Okay," Chris said, turning the speed to max. They took off, catching up with the ship in front of them in a matter of minutes. Soon, Chris was right where he needed to be. He was in the lead at last.

He went for what felt like a day or two without seeing anything. Then he realized that his training period was almost over. He decided that he had time to take a side trip to Neptune. First, he had to report in with the seniors in charge.

"This is Chris Johnson, aboard the scout ship Red Hawk. Everything's fine from up here, and I'm reaching the edge of the

It All Started In Chem Class...

solar system. I request permission to further explore Neptune for an undetermined amount of time, until the rest of the fleet catches up," he told the seniors.

"Permission granted," the leader said. Chris flew off-course and went around Neptune. He knew the simulation had to have some aliens programmed in it. He saw them as he came closer to the surface of the planet. A large colony of what seemed to be water-dwelling aliens. As far as Chris knew, Neptune was a completely gaseous planet. He called the seniors again.

"Colony spotted on the surface of Neptune. It's a fairly large colony," Chris said as he pulled up a scale map of the planet. This was one of the features Jordan had added for higher points. It took the approximate size of the planet as viewed by the people on board the ship, and compared it to the real size of the planet. From this, it could determine what a centimeter would be in actuality on the planet. "Maybe about a three-thousand-meter diameter. It appears to be a large circle of a slightly darker blue hue than the rest of the planet."

"Very well. We are shuttling a squad of EEU people over there as fast as we can. Orbit the planet for as long as your fuel will allow. We will send some extra fuel with the ship that brings them over. Have they made any apparent response to your presence near their planet?"

"None that I can tell." Chris zoomed in with the camera Jordan had provided him. He got down to what it would be like if he were just above the atmosphere. Then he saw an incredible sight. *Wow*, he thought. *They did a lot of work on this species.*

"Chris? What's going on?" Jordan was finally awake.

"They're sending an EEU team over. I found a colony on Neptune."

"Wow, nice work. Are they friendly?"

"I don't know yet. I'm looking for signs of life. Nice work on the zoom. Check this out. I can see what looks like hovering houses. The race of aliens is aquatic from the appearance of it. How long do you think the EEU guys are going to take?"

"You won't have to wait too long," Bob said, smiling. "What did you find? My team received some sort of urgent message. They figured it was nothing big, and sent me here."

"Well, look for yourself," Chris told him, motioning to the large screen.

"Hmmm. They seem to be aquatic, but that doesn't make any sense. Based on what I've read, they are highly advanced. The living structure is unrivaled on Earth. They are flying houses, which means either they have some sort of fantastic technology, or—"

"Or the houses are metallic, and the actual planet is a magnet as subzero temperature or something like that, right?" Chris was amazed that Jordan thought of all of that from floating houses.

"Something like that. Can you profile a specimen?"

"Yeah, but that's your job. I think they loaded these aliens to give you guys your sim work," Jordan said.

"Request permission to land," Bob said.

"I have the EEU guy, and he wants me to set her down," Chris told the senior ship.

"Permission granted. Be careful out there," he replied. When they landed on a floating landing strip, Chris and Jordan waived goodbye and walked out of the door. Suddenly, they found themselves back in the same training shuttle, but outside of the small cubicle they had been confined inside. Upon exiting the training ship, they saw the dean.

"Wow! That was fun, but I felt like I was in there for days," Chris said, stretching.

"Mr. Weendenahue, I'm quite surprised you slept as soundly as you did. I was never able to sleep that well. If you didn't have that water supply, you might have died. Actually, I doubt it, as you were only in there for three days," the dean said.

"Three days? You locked us up in there for three days?"

"Yes, Mr. Johnson, I did. I wanted you to adapt to being in a small space for a long time. See, since it was a simulation, you only *felt* like you were in there for three days, while you *thought*

It All Started In Chem Class...

that you were only in there for one day. Congratulations on beating the system, however. I will see you both on Friday. Now I suggest you both get back to your rooms and sleep in a nice, warm bed tonight," the dean replied. Chris hadn't even realized how tired he was until the dean said that. He barely made it back to his room before he fell asleep.

"All right, here's what I've got," Bob said once his group joined him in the sim chamber. "They appear to be highly advanced, and somehow aquatic."

"But Neptune is a gas giant," a sophomore said. "It's impossible to have an aquatic species on a gaseous planet!"

"Yeah, that's the point," a senior, who was leader of the Neptune squad, answered. "Well, see if they can communicate. How big are they?"

"About the size of a small monkey. They have feet, but then they also have fins and flippers and the like. I think they have mouths, but I know they have eyes. I'll try and talk to them," Bob answered. He walked up to one alien that was part of a large crowd that came to see them.

"Hello," he said to the alien. He didn't hear a reply. Rather, he felt one. *Hi*, the alien thought. *Telepathy*, John thought.

Very good.

Whoa! Sorry, I'm just not used to having people know exactly what I think, John thought, letting the alien "hear" him.

Well, tell your friends, the alien thought.

"Hey guys! They use telepathy!"

"Huh?" A cocky junior raised one eyebrow.

Yes, we do, the alien thought to everyone else in John's group. *We do not communicate in the simple method of vocal vibrations. Yes, we are far more advanced than you pathetic Homo sapiens, as you refer to yourselves. Because we have used incredible cloaking technology until now.* More aliens began to come out and meet the Earth people.

One person, who seemed to be a chief of sorts, thought up. *Yes, we are aquatic. We do have a liquid planet. It is made of things you can only imagine as gasses, but on our world, they are very much liquids. We would like you to know that we are a peaceful people. We are vegetarians, and we eat the food from the deepest of the depths. You would call them underwater plants, similar to the seaweed on your planet. Yes, we have been there, explored, and returned without your knowing. No, we will not come back with you! It has taken us millions of years to adapt to this planet and to this planet alone. We wouldn't live on your planet. Now, we will politely ask you to leave, or else.* He showed them a series of violent images to persuade them. They left without another word—or thought—to John.

"Finally! That sim is over," John said, breathing a sigh of relief.

"Even though they were computer generated, those things creeped me out," said a sophomore. They walked out the door, and got back into the training classroom.

The senior spoke to the dean. "Sir, we discovered upon arrival that they are a highly advanced—"

"Yes, I know. I watched you as you went through. Decent work. You may go. Training is dismissed for you." They left, all going their separate ways, with the senior in charge still muttering about "decent work? That's all we get?"

"Okay! It's time for those of you left to enter into the submersion room. All those majoring in matter teleportation, please go into the submersion room at this time. All you will be required to do is land ships, using such devices. You will have several large receiving ports that you will have to place on the surface of a planet. You will have several more dispensing ports that you will have to place on the ship. Sound easy? Well it's not!" The dean sat down and glanced at his watch after he finished the instructions.

Rich entered the room and went to the area with his name on it. He saw five replicas of his units. They started off by loading them on to shuttles, and sending them off to land. Once they landed, they added the dispensing ports. This was the hardest part of the sim. They had to put them on certain panels. They had to velcro them down. The panels would rise up and flip over,

It All Started In Chem Class...

exposing the panels to the outside. They would be activated by a robotic arm from the outside of the ship. It went Okay, for the most part. A couple of people had some trouble getting them buckled down, but in the end it worked.

The sim said that the ship was completely reconstructed, and it was all in working order. Then they had to do it again, on different terrain. They went through deserts, ice caps, grass, hills, and mountains. The mountains were really tricky. They had to get the receiving ports on at an angle, and then switch to that angle just before they initiated the teleportation.

Everyone had their training, and the dean felt they were ready for their mission. Chris and Jordan met John, Bob, and Rich as they came in. "How was training?" Chris yawned as he asked.

"Mine was easy enough," Rich said. "I just had to velcro on a port, and then take the other port and shuttle it to an imaginary planet. How was yours?"

"Except for the fact that I piloted the ship for *two entire days*, it went Okay," Chris replied. "Jordan took a nap and left me at the controls. The controls *he* designed, no less. How was yours?"

"Well," Bob said, "ours was weird. It had these messed-up aliens who didn't talk; they used telepathy. They said Neptune was water and all this weird stuff. Sim was fast though. At least that's good."

"I had to make gallons of that certain acid. It took a long time, but it sure beat flying a stationary craft!" Bob actually laughed at John's joke. Then, with the long days of grueling training over, Chris was ready to go to sleep.

"Good night! I think that now, for the first time in a long time, I can sleep soundly," he said. He was asleep by the time the words were out of his mouth. Everyone else followed his example, and went to sleep. Training was over, and the mission would begin the next day.

CHAPTER 17: THE DEEP-SPACE MISSION

"Time to go. Dean wants us there at 1000 hours today, guys," Rich said. They all got up, got ready, and went to the Café Probe.

"Whoa, Rich, I just got C-Mail from him! He says to bring . . our Spaceball stuff? That's weird. Oh, he says that we might want to practice, you know, keep our skills sharp. Rich, did you bring the MTU?" MTU was short for matter teleportation unit.

"I brought the receiving end. The other end is right under our Spaceball stuff. I thought about it before we left, just in case," he answered, smiling. With the flick of a button, their pads, helmets, and Spaceboards appeared.

"Thanks. You're a lifesaver," Chris told him.

"Yeah I know."

"I wasn't being serious, but oh well. Let's go!" After they ate more home-cooked meals for breakfast, they went to the docking bay, and saw, for the first time, the entire space fleet. "Wow," Chris said, "I designed more than half of them, and I'm still amazed!"

"Nice job," John told him. "Really impressive, isn't it?"

"Hey, let's find that one tile that's supposed to be off," Jordan said. They went over to about where it should be. Chris looked and looked. Then he realized what it was. He realized that's where the door to the shuttle was.

"Great," Bob said. "So that's the big deal, is it?"

"Okay, I was wrong. They didn't have that part drawn in to the model I saw. Hey, there's the dean! Everyone, be very hush-hush. Remember, I never saw anything."

"Stop being so concerned," Bob said. Then he cleared his throat. "Hey Dean, all ready for the big trip?"

"Shut up Bob, you sound like we're going camping," the dean replied irritably. "This *is* an important mission, for you especially."

"Why's that?"

"This will pull your grade out of the gutter," the dean answered.

"Oh. I'm *so glad* I got chosen," he said, not bothering to cover up the sarcasm in his voice.

"You should be!" The dean stalked away.

"Someone fell off the wrong side of his desk," Jordan said. They laughed.

"Hey, if I were the dean, I'd be mad every day of my life. I bet the doctor didn't have to smack his mom after he got to her," John said. Again, they laughed halfheartedly. Then, they took their bags to the vacuumation center. This is where they had all the air sucked out of their bags to make them smaller. After that, they put them in the Spacehaul truck. Spacehaul, the child company of U-Haul, was similar, but designed for use in space.

"Everyone will sit according to their majors and specialties within those majors. Chem students will sit in the back, then it will go as follows: Spaceship Design, Electronics, Matter Teleportation, and in the front will be Exploration and Explanation of the Unknown, as they will benefit from this in a great deal," said someone from SETI.

The dean came over to Chris's little circle. "Listen, you guys are prodigies. I know it. You are going to be the scout ship. The leader. All five of you will be one ship. It was designed, I believe, by you, Chris."

"I designed one a while back, but I never showed it to anyone," Chris replied.

"Well, your teacher received it via C-Mail, and we constructed it a couple months of ago. SETI has used it once or twice, and it runs very well. That is why we are using it. I trust you five for several reasons. First, Chris designed this ship, and he knows every nook and cranny. I know you are the only people who would fly with him. John, you are specializing in acid, which would be useful. What you can do is dissolve things before we get there. And also, I wouldn't recommend the whole 'glass missile' concept. Just make large jets so that it covers a large area. Jordan, we used one of your systems, because as I recall, you designed something for a scout ship. Now, Rich, you probably won't have very much to do, because the scout ship won't be landing. Bob, you will notify some people higher up if you see anything that looks suspicious. You will leave first, and travel at a constant speed. Chris, I did rig it so that you cannot exceed that speed unless necessary. I have entered a code that your cracker doesn't even know exists. Anyway, get going!"

Chris noticed the ship. It was exactly like he designed it. "There's the ship. So, which one of you C-Mailed the design?"

"It was him," they all said in unison, pointing at two other people.

"See, if only four of you had lied, I would have known. Having *all* of you lie makes it really difficult. Don't worry though, because this was my luxury model. It has synthetically enhanced leather. Get this: the temperature of the leather cools or warms depending on the temperature of your body. I got an HTV with a D3D player and satellite dish. We get to travel in style. Odd thing is, that design had about five other scout ships that were a lot better for just work and stuff. They picked the luxury vehicle. Oh well. And also, I have a fold-out king bed in the back. It has a washer and dryer, all kinds of things. Uh, the ship, not the bed," he added as he noticed Rich looking at the bed.

"Nice. How many nights of sleep did you lose?" Bob didn't know how Chris stayed up so late, and still did stuff like that.

"Not nearly as many as you," Chris responded. He sat in the driver's seat, admiring his controls. "Jordan, how do these work?"

"Pretty simple. The steering wheel steers like any normal wheel, but it can move up and down, adjusting altitude. There's the 3D monitor where the dean or anyone else on the mission can contact us. Those right there are your gauges. Now, we just wait for the message from the dean," Jordan said. After a few minutes, they got what they wanted.

"All right, gentlemen. Time to go. You are cleared for takeoff," the dean instructed them.

It All Started In Chem Class...

"Jordan, you forgot something," Chris said, glancing around.

"What did I forget?"

"How do I turn it on?"

"Oops. Hit the little yellow button in the corner," he answered, embarrassed.

"Jordan, why do you always have to be so different? I mean, why isn't it the green button in the middle? Too cliché?" Chris pushed the button, and felt the motors hum to life. He turned the lever to full power, and shot out like a bullet.

"Actually, that's exactly right," Jordan replied.

"Whatever. Buckle your seatbelts, please secure all carry-on baggage, and hold on to your hats," Chris yelled as he flew out the hatch. Then, he hit the DEAN button on his fleet-monitor. "Hey Dean! What's up?"

"Chris? What are you doing?"

"Making sure my equipment works! Hey, where exactly do you want me to fly?"

"We are supposed to explore a rumored tenth planet. "

"Don't fly near Mars or anything?"

"No. We need to get there. You can just put it in cruise, and do hovercrafting or whatever you call those weird things," the dean said, sighing.

"All right. Thanks, Dean. See you later," Chris told him, hitting the button. Then, over the intercom, he said, "Good afternoon. My name is Chris Johnson and I will be your pilot. I would like to remind you that even though we are in space, there will still be gravity as long as the apple light is on. I would also like to ask that you leave your seatbelt on until the seatbelt light is turned off."

"Chris, give it a rest," Rich said.

"Ok. But seriously, we will be approaching Mars in about three hours. That will give us some gravitational trouble, but I'll pull us out, no problem. After that, we're going way off to the left so that I can avoid Jupiter's field. At some point, I'm gonna put on cruise control and then get some sleep. Kitchen and bathrooms are in the back."

Chris just settled back in his chair and watched the Earth, the moon, the station, and the large red planet that loomed in front of him. He turned on the HTV and watched some digitalized classics. Some of the greatest movies of all time had been rewritten in D3D code. The driving for him was fairly simple, as it was a few hours between each large body.

Rich knew exactly what he wanted to do. He had to get up early that day, and wanted to make up for lost sleep. He lay down on the bed, and was asleep before he got to the first sheep.

John listened to his personal SM radio. SM was the radio used in space, because it went to a satellite, which provided great reception wherever he was in orbit. He even got frequencies for commercial-free stations. His SM was like his best friend.

Jordan was trying to figure out how to burn his own D3Ds. With all his electronics knowledge, he thought it would be simple. After he started working on it, he realized it was a long, time-consuming project. He was happy, though, because it gave him something to do on the shuttle mission.

Bob played around with his EEU devices, trying to see what different aliens would look like. He would enter random information, like "aquatic species," "has wings," "has long red hair," and see what the computer could generate. It came up with some freakish designs. He had fun trying to get various data errors.

Chris had about an hour of free time, in which he watched a movie and enjoyed the comforts of technology. He still loved the synthetically enhanced seats he had.

At the moment they were room temperature, because his body was right at the perfect temperature. As he came upon Mars, he turned gently to the left. He passed somewhat close to the surface, and looked down at the deep red of the planet. There was something all-out calming about it.

It All Started In Chem Class…

Now came the tricky part. "John, get working on those acid jets. I might have to take out an asteroid or two along the way," Chris said.

"Whatever. You're the boss," John replied. John started working as Chris entered the asteroid belt.

"Well, do you guys think I should clear out any asteroids? Or let those seniors maneuver on their own?"

"Blast out a couple big ones," Jordan replied. Chris darted around several smaller asteroids, making a couple of very near misses. It was easy, because the ship handled very well. It wasn't as good as his other designs, but it handled like a dream.

"Okay, here's the stuff," John told him as he got out the acid. Chris took it and loaded into the spray-jet canisters the dean had given him, and put those into their holsters in the ship.

"I think I'll take out that one," Chris said. He pointed to a large asteroid, and hit the SPRAY ONE button. He aimed it, and it looked like he was dosing it with a large bottle of hair spray. But, instead of stiffening it, the solution dissolved it upon impact. Then, he noticed a huge chunk of space rock in front of him. He hit the SPRAY TWO button, and swerved to the left to avoid coming in contact with it.

"Okay, we will be experiencing a slight amount of turbulence. I will have to turn on the seatbelt light at this time. We will be out of the asteroid belt in about half an hour, so if you would please remain seated until that time, thank you," Chris told his passengers. As they went, his ship was struck by several smaller asteroids that did little more than scratch.

"Dean Picklodgicer, I took out two of the largest asteroids. The acid went straight through them. I'll be here for another thirty minutes or so," he told the dean.

"Okay, good work. After this, you will want to veer off to the left and stay there for some time. That's when you can really hit the cruise button," replied the dean.

"Okey dokey. Bye, dean." Chris continued along the same path, swerving to avoid the asteroids. Soon, he was out of the asteroid belt. "Big turn coming up," he said, right before making a turn that send them a long way from the straight path they were keeping.

"Why are we doing this again? Jupiter's gravity?" Rich had just woken up, and forgot what they were doing.

"Something like that. Anyway, at least it will keep us alive."

"All right," Rich said sleepily. Instead of going to sleep, he got up and watched a D3D for a while.

"Man, I've never been this close to Jupiter before," Bob commented, awestruck. "I mean, the big red spot looks so tiny on the pictures. Seeing it in real life is so much cooler."

"Yeah, I can get you a larger image of it if you want," Chris replied.

"Sure, that sounds cool." Chris keyed in and pulled up an enhanced image of the big red spot. It was indeed just a large spiraling hurricane.

"Wow. That's the only way to describe this. Aren't we the first people to come this close to it? This is so much cooler than the Grand Canyon," Rich said. They all stared at it for a while, before Chris regained his senses.

"Uh-oh," he said.

"What's wrong?"

"Meet Ganymede," the pilot told Jordan. "Get back in your seats and buckle your seat belts. I'm gonna have to pull a vert." Vert was a slang term for going straight up, a shortened form of the word vertical. They all ran back and put on their seatbelts. As soon as they did, Chris slammed the steering wheel up, so that the ship was turned on its back and went straight up in the air. As soon as they were clear of Ganymede, Chris slammed it back into a flat position.

"Geez Chris, don't go that fast!"

"Sorry John, but I couldn't see Ganymede. Anyway, Saturn is still about five hours off, so I'm gonna catch my beauty sleep."

"Yeah," Rich said dryly, "we all know you need it." Chris ignored him and jumped into his bed. Within minutes he was asleep.

"Hey guys," John asked them, "could I get this thing to move at all?"

"No," Jordan replied shortly. They resumed whatever it was they were doing before they got to Jupiter. Jordan was still working on his own personal D3D burner.

"Hey Rich, if I could get a file on my holocomp into D3D format, I could hypothetically burn it, right?"

"Sure, I guess. You're the big electronics genius, not me."

"Okay, I'll try it."

"What good would that do us, anyway?"

"Well, we could rent D3Ds and then copy them."

"Ooh, get to work man!" The ship went straight without any problems. Chris slept through everything that happened, but nothing really did. Chris slept all the way until the dean called about four hours after their encounter with Ganymede.

"Anything up ahead we need to worry about?"

"Might wanna watch out for Ganymede while you're sightseeing. We did a zoom-in on the big red spot. That thing is cool up close. Other than Ganymede, we haven't hit any problems. It's really fairly simple. So, should we look for anything from here 'til Pluto?"

"Nope, you're clear 'til then. Did I interrupt your nap?"

"Yeah, how'd you know?"

"I installed a camera, just to check. Jordan, I'm going to have to add a D3D copier policy to our rules."

"Oh great. Hey Dean, time we get back, I'll be done!" Jordan laughed at the image of the flustered dean. Then he dropped the project on the floor.

"Well, I hope you learned *your* lesson," the dean replied smirking.

"I'll get you back; just wait." Jordan picked up the half-finished copier. "Hey look, Dean! Nothing damaged! Who could've imagined?"

"Oh well, I have to check on the normal ships now," he said, putting emphasis on normal. Then his image disappeared.

"Do you think he was serious about that D3D thing?"

"Jordan, don't worry about it," Chris told him, sighing. "If he does, who cares? They might search the room, but I doubt it. Just get back to work. I figure about 10 hours or so until we get there. I'm just gonna watch the old holovision. Talk to you later. By the way, is anyone gonna make us some space food?"

"Probably," John said. "I took a cooking course in Chem. Pretty fun, and they teach you how to make soup that tastes like steak and stuff. Right out of 'Wonka: 50th Anniversary in 3D.' I'll work on it. The other thing is I have access to an excess of the ingredients to make it, so I can make like ten times the normal amount. I'll get to work on it."

"Ok." Chris turned on the television and started watching some sitcom; he didn't even know the name of it. It was funny, though, and it passed the time. Chris enjoyed space travel the first time he tried it, but after a while it became boring. The part he really hated was just plain going. You couldn't feel the floating sensation as long as you were accelerating. Fortunately, he still got to be weightless due to the speed limit the dean set on the craft. Everyone did, as soon as Chris turned off the gravity field. It took them by surprise, and soon they were all floating in the air.

"Chris! A warning would be nice," Rich yelled.

"So would a quadrillion dollars. Which do you think will happen first?" Rich didn't answer, he knew it was a rhetorical question. He had been on missions with Chris, and knew he never turned on the gravity field with a fair warning.

Chris watched HTV while John made his great tasting dinner. Jordan was still working hard on his D3D burner/copier. Rich had fun teleporting things onto people's backs and back again. Bob spent his time reading some book by Shakespeare; he didn't know what it was, but he liked all the fights and deaths. He only read it because he heard it involved double suicide. This was the way things went along for a few hours. They glanced out the window as they reached Saturn.

It All Started In Chem Class...

"Chris, get me a close-up on those rings," Bob requested.

"Sure," Chris answered. He keyed in a close up of the rings. They sat and watched them turn for a long time. Chris realized that the beautiful spectrum was about to be over, while everyone else just gazed. There was just something about seeing something that incredible that close that gave them all a sense of awe.

"Well that makes six planets down and three to go until the real mission starts," Rich commented.

"Yeah, something like that," Chris replied. "Hey John, is the magic formula done yet?"

"Nah, it takes a while to like, I dunno, make the magic that makes it taste like meat. All I know is the recipe calls it to sit for two hours. I guess that's when the juices ferment," he said, shrugging.

"Dude you never told me it was alcoholic!"

"Geez, Chris, it's not alcoholic. It's just an expression, you know? I mean, that's what gives them the right stuff to taste good or something like that."

"Oh, okay. Because I was gonna say, if it *is* alcoholic, then we can't let the dean see it," Chris replied with an ear-to-ear grin. Then, the dean popped up on the holovision, and Chris just hit the "SHUT THE DEAN UP" button. "Thanks for that one, Jordan."

"No problem. Remember that benefits me as much as it does you. What planet's next on the solar system tour?"

"Whoa! We're up to Neptune. Man, time flies when you're making the dean mad."

"Yeah, you're right. I never would've guessed we were that far already," Bob replied.

"One more planet until we reach," Chris paused as he hit the dean's button, "what is that planet called?"

"Planet X, named of course after the Roman numeral for ten. Your mission will be to orbit it as I give you information. It will be a fair ways off. In fact, I suggest you all sleep on the quadruple bunk beds and leave one person keeping watch."

"For once I'm actually going to take that advice. Goodnight."

"Goodnight Chris, everyone," John said.

"Well, I'll take some responsibility and take first watch," Rich said sarcastically. But he was serious because he sat in the copilot's seat, watching the radar and other instruments necessary to their survival. Everyone else climbed into the four beds that folded out of the walls and went to sleep. Every hour, they switched watches. Nothing very interesting happened for a very long time. The most excitement was when the dean called them for an update.

"How are things?"

"Boring as ever, Dean. Can't we speed up just a little bit?"

"Actually, the speed I gave you has put you well ahead of us. We are just now approaching Jupiter. I'm going to decrease max speed and let you all get some sleep. I'm well protected, so I'll watch your ship and notify you of anything," the dean told Jordan, who was on the fifth watch.

"Thanks Dean. Actually though, I think it's about time for us to eat." Then, to John he said, "Hey man! Isn't it time for dinner yet?"

John rubbed the sleep out of his eyes. "Yeah, I think. I'll go check it." He walked over to the blue liquid meal. "Everyone ready for dinner?"

"Huh? Whoa, what time is it?" They all answered in unison, and slight variations of what Chris asked.

"Shift number five, I think," John said sleepily.

"No, I'm on my second shift, so this is number ten. Dean says they are *way* behind," Jordan answered, extending the "way" for several seconds. "He's gonna lower our max speed." Then he hit the "TELL THE DEAN TO SHUT UP" button.

"Yes?"

"Dean Picklodgicer, we can't lower the speed. We've all had eight hours of sleep and are about to eat dinner. Breakfast. Whatever you want to call it, we're about to eat it."

It All Started In Chem Class...

"Very well. I'm going to send ahead another ship to give us an updated report of what's going on ahead of us. It's a fast ship so it might be able to catch up with you. Of course, everyone will be around Planet X, because you will be in orbit the whole time."

"Thanks Dean!" Then Jordan hit the "NO MORE DEAN" button. Everyone was thrown off by the sudden increase in speed. John served them steak soup, and they all ate it very quickly. Everyone was starved from a long time of fasting.

"Whoa! This soup is awesome! Man, I've never tasted any real steak this good."

"Well thanks. By the way, has anyone seen my arsenic?"

"Hahaha, but sorry dude, we've heard the old arsenic-in-the-chem-soup joke. That one's nothing new," Bob said.

"Oh well. I'll get you next time."

"Hey, who wants to start a pool tournament?"

"Chris, how many times do I have to beat you before you realize I'm better?"

"Actually, I had hoped to play Bob first this time." Even in space you could play pool. They even developed what they called telescoposticks, which were sticks that flew out from a chamber about thirty centimeters long. This would result in a full-length pool stick that could fit in any pool junkie's pocket. Chris's luxury ship had a pool table that was in an underground chamber. After you hit a secret switch, it would flip out and raise itself, balls in order and ready for breaking.

"Okay I'll play you," Bob replied. They played an entire tournament, and another and then yet another. It was a good way to pass time, and it made everyone better players.

"Hey, I think we should practice some Spaceball!"

"Bob, how can we? And besides, why would it even matter?"

"I don't know, but come on, let's try the three doors run. Chris, fold out all this stuff," he said.

"Okay," Chris responded as he hit a switch on the wall that made most everything flip back into holding chambers. Then, he got out all the Spaceball equipment and they got it on.

"Okay, Bob, how do we do the three doors run?" Rich had heard of it, but never before had he tried to run it.

"Okay, three people--you, John, and me--will fly out. One of us will have the Spaceball. The other team has to try and guess which 'door' it's behind. If they guess it correctly, we fly as fast as we can. If they guess it incorrectly, then we get a free shot at the Abyss. Most teams play along. Chris and Jordan, you get to be the other team."

"Bob, that's the dumbest idea I've ever heard. Let's just do a plain circle run," Rich suggested. They all agreed, and began to fly around in circles with the gravity field off. They hit the ball from person to person. After a while of doing this, they switched to an Indian Run, where one person had to constantly fly up to the front of the line. When they came by the control console, Chris checked the radar.

"Hey, there's a ship behind us by about twenty million or so," Chris said.

"Cool. That's too far to contact, right?"

"Yes, and at this rate, they won't be within contact range until we reach Planet X, which is still . . ." he stopped, because he was amazed at what his holocomp readouts were telling him.

"What's wrong?"

"It's twenty minutes off, Rich! Twenty minutes and all of this traveling will have been worth something! Everyone, forget Spaceball; I'm gonna have myself some fun flying for once! Buckle your seatbelts, because I'm gonna give us some serious turbulence!" Chris put on his best fighter pilot face, strapping himself in as they all did what he requested, and very quickly too, because he started swerving all around. Chris had so much fun that he forgot to look for Planet X.

"Chris man! Watch out! It's right there!"

"Thanks Rich!" Chris immediately slowed down and pulled over to the large cloud of asteroids that would point the way to PlanetX.

CHAPTER 18: PLANET X

"Chris, can you make it through that cloud of asteroids?"

"Yeah. This wasn't in the sim, but I've done things like this before," he replied, with false confidence. He wasn't quite sure if he could or not. He had designed the ship with fair armor, but it was a complete cloud of asteroids, orbiting around the planet.

"That is one big planet," John said.

"Yeah," Rich agreed. "Chris, is there any way to see what's behind the asteroids?"

"None at all." Chris hit the dean button again. "Dean, we're at Planet X. Do you want us to attempt entry through the asteroid field or orbit around?"

"Orbit around for now. I'm going to give you some information about the planet. It was conceptualized in the late 20th Century. Its existence was only proven about five years ago. You aren't actually the first people to go there. In fact, ever since we developed deep-space shuttles like this one, people have been making many visits here. Every so often, the elliptical orbit of Pluto throws off some of the asteroids, giving you a fifteen-second window in which you can get through. We estimate the next one to be occurring very soon. Get ready. Find Pluto on the radar, and wait until it passes close to Planet X and then fly through. I will provide you with more information upon your arrival on the planet. Actually, a separate crew will be there to welcome you. Roughly ten seconds to the opening."

Chris tensed at the controls. Then, suddenly, he saw asteroids "pulled" off by Pluto. He knew, however, that wasn't what really happened.

"Anyone else see the rockets on those?"

"Not now, Bob! I've got to take my opportunity." Chris threw the wheel down, literally. He dropped to the proper entry level in five seconds. Then he had ten left to maneuver inside. He still couldn't see anything on the other side. He swerved around several more projecting asteroids. Then, he saw the window in perfect clarity. He just realized that his speed max had increased drastically. He floored it, giving him about ten gs of force. He thought his cheeks would be ripped off his cheekbones. Then he was in, and had to stop suddenly.

"Dean, that's no planet," Bob said. "What is it?"

"Don't worry about that. Just find a good place to land." The sight in front of them was stunning. It was no planet, rather a large metallic sphere floating in space. It had windows and such, but it was mostly metal. Chris saw the docking bay. And that's exactly what it was. A docking bay, similar to the one on the space station, but with a large number of large ships. Chris had no trouble landing.

"Bring the Spaceball stuff or else we'll explode," Rich reminded them, over-exaggerating for sarcasm. The docking bay was the only part of the "planet" that was exposed to the harsh climate, or void thereof, of space. So, they got out, with Spaceball stuff in hand, and made their way to the glass door at the other end.

"Hello, gentlemen, and welcome to Planet X."

"What's up with all of this? And who are you?" Rich still wasn't used to it all, and got a little irritated.

"I am the construction chief here. Actually, I *was*. Construction is complete."

"You mean you built this planet?"

"Yes, and you may call me Will or Mr. Will or simply sir," Will said. "And I'm also very glad to see that you are equipped for Spaceball."

"Why is that?"

"Ah, Chris, the captain. Fireblast, correct? Yes, I must admit that I follow Spaceball. That's why I was so excited that I got this project."

"What the heck is Planet X?"

"Well I guess you figured out it's not really a planet. When we first developed deep-space travel, this was our first project. Originally, it was going to be a radio broadcaster to search for extraterrestrials. Then, once we invented Spaceball, we being the people of Earth and Space, we decided that no one really got the

It All Started In Chem Class...   125

effect in a semispherical arena. So, we decided to change this place into a spherical Spaceball arena. From now on, this is where the championship games will be held."

"So *that's* why Dean Picklodgicer wanted us to come! We're in the finals! And so is that other team that came!"

"Yes, very good, John, and also, if you noticed, many Spaceball players were taken on this mission. Of course, the nerds came to keep up appearances."

"And what about the asteroids?"

"Ah, hello, Iceman. Well, that kept it a complete secret. Yes, those were projections of asteroids. We plan to stop the sphere totally, and that will be the grand unveiling. It will be incredible. And, as the only unbeaten team as of yet, you will get to cut the giant ribbon. Well, what do you think?"

"W-w-w-w-w-w-w-w-w-w-wow," Jordan replied with wide eyes.

"Yes, that's quite how I felt," Will said.

"Couldn't have said it better myself," Chris commented.

"So, can we go in?"

"Sure, Mr. Cashed-Out. I'll give you the grand tour. First stop is the entry hall." He waited to let them ooh and ah at the incredible scoreboards, HTVs and chairs set up around the room. Subsequently, he led them on to the ticket room which was empty, because no one knew about the arena yet. Then, he took them into one of the seating sections. There were seats up and down the sides. They had them all around, all the way up until the angle became too intense for someone to take. Everyone was protected by super-strength glass.

"Now, these are the seats. See, the nice thing about space is that we turn off the g-forces to let people get to their seats, and turn them on once they're in it. Don't worry; there are platforms that come out to protect them from a free-fall. Now there are elevators here that you can't see, to take you to your locker rooms." He reached out and grabbed the glass, which was apparently a handle. They all walked into the elevator, and went to their locker rooms.

"How many years are we going to be here?" Chris asked, because they had incredibly lush accommodations.

"Just a couple of months," Will replied. "The teachers wouldn't let us have it any sooner than the last day because of finals. The whole college is coming to watch. I'll leave you here to let it all soak in. The other team will come down to meet you in about five minutes."

Will left them with so many questions. The other team came down, and they talked for a while. Both teams were completely amazed. Chris was still so stunned that he forgot to answer his phone.

"Hello?"

"Hello Chris. What do you think?"

"Dean Picklodgicer! Well sir, quite frankly, we're in shock. This place is awesome! And we still have two months before we play?"

"Actually, Will was misinformed. We've changed that. You play tomorrow. Today you can rest. Tomorrow, you will practice and then play. Enjoy your stay on Planet X!" Chris hung up, and laid down on his huge silk bed. He was so overwhelmed he wasn't sure which way was up. Chris, and everyone else with him, drank some soda, and—despite the caffeine and sugar—faded out to sleep.

CHAPTER 19: THE GRAND OPENING

"Good morning everyone!"

"Goo—what time is it?"

"Good morning Chris, Will," John said. "Will, Chris doesn't like being awakened at, well, what time is it, anyway?"

"1000 hours," Will replied. "Out here, it's never really light, because we're so far away from the sun. That's why you slept so well. Anyway, do you guys want the first or second four-hour practice session?"

"Chris, you decide," Rich said.

"Second sound okay with everyone?"

"Yeah," they replied in unison.

"Okay then! Be out there at 1400 hours," Will said, smiling. He left, and they began to get ready.

"One more thing! The grand unveiling is in two hours. Do you all want to cut the ribbon, or just let one of you?"

"Chris can," John said.

"We all can," Chris replied.

"Okay then. Get ready by high noon," Will responded with a laugh, since the sun was much smaller, and didn't arc across the sky during the game. Then, he left them alone to get ready. Two hours later, they were out in the stands, about to go to the top of the planet. "Glad you could make it," Will told them.

"Wouldn't have missed it for the world," Rich said. They took their positions.

"We're live in 5...4...3," the cameraman started.

"Hello. I am the dean of the International Space Station and University. I broadcast today from atop 'Planet X,' a secret experiment, designed to revolutionize the sport of Spaceball. Yes, this is the fabled planet. The truth is, this is the Spaceball arena. We are going to open ticket sales today for the first-ever match played here, between Team Alpha-Beta-Nu and Team Delta-Delta-Delta a.k.a. Team D^3. Both are incredible teams and are supported by the school. At the college, we fully support all forms of athletics, which include Spaceball, Spaceball, and yes, you guessed it, Spaceball. It is a hugely popular sport in space, and also on Earth. However, since the start of Spaceball, the only people lucky enough to attend were those of us already in space. We have created several ships large enough to carry four hundred people, and also make it here in less than a day. The seating capacity here is roughly seventy-five thousand people. This is the first and most likely the only match where tickets will be sold on Earth. You will also have to pay for your shuttle tickets to get here. Tickets are on sale now at all major ticket retailers. Well, I know you don't want to hear me ramble, so I'll stop now, and give you *the greatest team ever! Team D-3.* They are: Chris Johnson, the captain, John Smith, Bob Tankalova, Rich Flithinteon, and Jordan Weendenahue. Now, here is Chris Johnson," he announced.

"Thanks Dean. I'm Chris, and we're the team. It's really an honor to be playing the first-ever game here. This is a great team, and these are great people. I don't know anyone I'd rather share this honor with. My team, holding a super-sized pair of scissors, is going to cut the large ribbon that holds shut the doors of the arena. According to the dean, the ships will leave Earth in about ten minutes. We wanted to have something of a crowd here, but, oh well! Let's get this started."

Chris and everyone else grabbed the giant pair of scissors and cut the ribbon. Those who had come with them cheered and screamed, even though no one could hear them. "Ladies and gentlemen, I give you *Planet X*. We will commence the game upon arrival and settling in of the crowd. What's this? What? Am I hearing this correctly? We're already sold out of tickets! I don't believe this! Folks, please, I'm sorry, but *don't try and buy tickets; we're sold out!* Back to you Dean," Chris finished with vigor. They went back inside.

CHAPTER 20: THE FINALS

After four hours of boring but intense practice, Chris and the rest of Team D^3 were ready for what had to have been the biggest Spaceball game ever. As Chris looked out during a short rest, he saw that the seventy-five thousand people were all there, every single one of them.

"Hey Chris, we never got our new boards, did we?"

"Rich, it's a little late now," Chris replied, sighing.

"I know," he said as he drew out 4 Nitro 24-cylinder engines powering five brand-new, top-of-the-line, waxed boards complete with the D^3 logo on it and a picture of a Flamethrower.

"Dude, didn't we pick those up at the shop?"

"No, we got an older model, but that was similar. Problem was it was an external combustion engine. Now they've made a newer model, and get this: each board is a signature board for each of us. They each have our own personal nickname engraved on our board. Each board is also designed with a different mold based on personal performances in our previous matches and on different boards. They went all out on this one. Best part is, if we win, they're *completely free!*" Everyone cheered.

"All right! Now listen, I know you want those boards, and you all know I want mine for free, so go out there and *win*! You don't want to see those price tags, and worse than that is going to be my face if we lose. Now, are we going to lose?"

"I hope not!" John exclaimed..

"No, sir," Bob replied with a salute.

"Bob, shut up. Chris, why would we lose now?" Rich always thought Chris was a little over-zealous about Spaceball.

"We haven't lost. Neither has the other team. This is gonna be without animals. Yes, 5-on-5 Spaceball. Hey whoa, they even included the DDD pad! Now, let's go get used to these." They flew out of the hatch, much to the approval of the crowd. Chris was glad to see Wedgeheads, who wore large green wedges on their heads to show support for the team. Chris saw some people wearing the traditional red of the ABN team. Chris flew up to the ref.

"Okay gentlemen, you all know the rules. I want a good clean game. This time, due to the larger arena, we're giving you a larger time limit. Ninety minutes will be allowed to score as many goals as you possibly can. There are now four Abysses--one at the top, bottom, left side, and right side. Today, we will use a specially designed quarter, with an emblem of three triangles on the heads side and ABN in red on the tails side. Team D-3, you may call it in the air." They moved into the stands. The ref flipped the coin.

"*Heads!*"

"I'm sorry, but the answer we were looking for is tails. Team ABN, do you want to take it or give it?"

"We will give it away," the captain, named Jeff, said.

"Chris, man, that's not good; that's not good at all; that's very, very bad," John told him.

"Dude, we've never tried this before," Rich commented.

"I know. They've watched our videos, and they think this is going to throw off our plan. But we all know that's not going to happen, right?"

"Okay, Chris, which two goals are you going to take? They are left, right, top, and bottom," the ref said as he indicated with his hand.

"Top and left," Chris replied seeing nods of agreement from his team.

"Very well. Begin!"

"Yeah, right," Jordan said. "So Chris, we're about to get it. What do we do?"

"Okay, we have to throw them off. I'm gonna do a fake catch with you and Bob. Bob, we're going to set up in a basic star formation, you central. The minute it's in the space, you and Jordan switch places. They won't get it. They aren't going to know why we're doing it. Set up, let's go!" They set up in the star formation, and the Spaceball was thrown. As soon as it was, the other team took off, going right for Bob. As soon as he and Jordan

It All Started In Chem Class...

started to switch, Chris and Bob closed in to head them off. Jordan caught it and took off.

"Okay, no coach here, what do I do?"

"Go straight up, everyone else go down behind him just a little bit. Jordan, fake it to me. I'm going to pass you. As soon as you fake it, veer off to the left. They know that I'm more comfortable going up. I love having both goals. Let's do it!" Chris took off, soaring above Jordan, while Bob, Rich, and John went behind him, fending off anyone from the other team. Jordan slipped the ball into his right hand, and made a throwing motion with his left. He swerved off to the left, and everyone followed Chris. Everyone except Brian, the other captain. Fortunately, Jordan had a head start. He and Chris were both sitting at the Abysses.

"Hey Chris, we never did find out what's at the bottom of the Abyss," Jordan said.

"Let's do it! But Brian's got your tail. How you going to shake him off?"

"I had planned to ask Bob for some help," he said.

"On my way," Bob said as he dropped down.

"Ah, so Chris, you were just a decoy, weren't you?"

"Not at all," Chris said as he danced around the Abyss.

"Then why are you protecting Jordan?"

"I want everyone playing at their best," he said. Bob hit the tail of Brian's board, sending him flying upward. "Actually, maybe I was the decoy," Chris replied mockingly as Jordan threw in the Spaceball for the first point of the game.

"But you never play twins!"

"Yeah. After we saw you give us the ball we kinda figured you'd know all our moves, so we tried some new stuff. Thought it might just throw you off your game."

"Good job."

"No offense, but it's gotta feel bad to find out that we're two steps ahead of the people who are one step ahead of us."

"Yep," Brian said. "Well, if you keep doing everything you've never done, I suppose that beating you will be rather hard."

"That's the general idea, all right," Bob said. "By the way, Jordan's about to—"

"Start wondering where you are," Chris said, to keep Brian's mind off the game.

"Chris, really, it's Okay, I know that we're about to get the Spaceball. I've got a four-man game lined up for you," Brian replied with a grin.

"Brian, you always do a four-man game after the first move to the Abyss," Chris said with a sigh. "Team, get ready for a three-man game. Brian wants me to think they'll play four, so they won't. I don't know who will be part of the run, so take your man to the edge. Got it?"

"Man, my guy's so small I could take three of him," Rich said.

"Don't underestimate small people. If he weaves in and out or something like that, and you let him—"

"Chris I get the idea. Let's go!" Rich threw the Spaceball and took off. He threw it to his own man, and then chased after him. "Nice try."

"I'm afraid I don't follow you," the other guy said.

"Chris, he is *wide* open! He wants me to think he'll take it all the way. I think it will go to Brian but I'm not sure. You wanna cover him?"

"Jordan, watch their captain, Brian, okay? Everyone else, follow him. Jordan, fake a faulty engine or something."

"Got it!" Chris, Bob, John, and Rich all took off after one person. "Chris, what happens if it doesn't go to Brian?"

"Trouble," Chris said with a sigh. Jordan hung back, keeping a fair distance between himself and Brian, and a shorter distance between himself and the Abyss.

"Three-man ball, remember?"

"Thanks Bob. That guy over there; his name is Alan and he's fading off. Take him out."

"Gotcha," Bob said, already moving off towards Alan, baton at his side.

It All Started In Chem Class...   133

"So, Chris, is it going to be Alan or is it going to be me? You have to have a main focus, you know," Brian taunted. As he spoke, Jordan flew up behind him with his new baton raised. Then Chance, who had the Spaceball following Jordan's score, threw the Spaceball right at Jordan's baton. Brian got the signal and ducked, grabbing the Spaceball. He took off with Jordan right behind him.

"Not today," Jordan screamed as he slammed his baton on Brian's board. Brian did exactly as Bob had planned; he threw the Spaceball to Alan just as Bob slammed down Alan's board with his elbow.

"Ow, I hit my funny bone!"

"Oh yeah? I'm gonna hurt a whole lot more than that! Give me back that Spaceball!"

"Sorry, buddy, I don't have it," Bob said laughing. Bob flew in literal circles.

"Well, if you don't have it, and I don't have it, then who does?" Suddenly, panels were removed to allow the smoke machines to pour fog into the arena. As they opened, Brian looked at his watch, and realized that he only had twenty minutes left to play. When the panels were removed, shouts could be heard.

"Cashed Out!" was the cry heard from around the stands. Rich had the ball, with John, Chris, and Jordan flying around him. The fans continued to scream "Cashed Out! Cashed Out! Cashed Out!"

"Hey Brian, you wanted to play four-man, right? Well," Chris said with a sigh, "you're playing it." Infuriated by Chris's comments, the other team charged faster than they should have. "Rich, do it!"

"Whatever happened to stall-out-burn-out?" Stall-out-burn-out was a term for stalling in a game that was originally used to burn out the other team's engines.

"*Forget I said it!*"

"That works for me," Rich answered as he began spiraling down into the Abyss. He knew that soon the polarity switcher-upper, as it was commonly called, would attempt to mess him up. Fortunately, using a move he had reviewed on the trip, he moved the board side-to-side and spiraled simultaneously, creating something that would counter the powers of the polarity switcher-upper.

"Okay, circle up around the Abyss," Chris told his team.

"But," John asked, "what about the polarity switcher-upper?"

"If we cover like a five-man free-for-all, we won't have any trouble. Jordan, time check!"

"Half over," he said. They all assembled into the free-for-all motion, and began spinning rapidly, after further instructions from Chris.

"Chris, we're gonna shoot right through the old stupid circle-the-pit formation!"

"Okay Brian, I'll be waiting," Chris replied. Then, to Rich, he said, "I'm going to hold them off as long as I can. All you have to worry about is being ready to throw it in at a moment's notice, okay?"

"I'm fine. Just stall out if you can." Chris and the rest of the team continued to circle the Abyss, batons ready. The other team charged closer and closer, without raising their batons. They formed into a line of four, with Brian behind. "Jordan, what's Brian's game?" Jordan had seen several tapes of the other team.

"I have no idea," he replied, shaking his head. The four teammates in a line ran right into Chris's spiraling pattern, but Brian paused. Then he unsnapped his baton and threw it through the small gap, hitting the firewall switch.

"Get away," Chris told them.

"Chris, what's going on? Oh, I see," Rich sighed, he flew down in the same pattern, and waited right at the brink of the Abyss. As soon as the other team came over the top, he flew down right in to the Abyss, because the machine that would pull the Spaceball the last three meters was turned off on two goals for the finals. This meant he had to fly down until he could trap the Spaceball to score. His board was easily beating the other team's as far as speed was concerned, but he lacked an extended overdrive switch. *When will this end? It just seems to go on and on forever,*

It All Started In Chem Class...

Rich thought to himself. As he passed another turn, he still saw no sign of light.

"Rich, what's going on down there?"

"John, these Abysses are specially made with all these turns and stuff!"

"Oh, I see. Look, I got an idea. It's risky, but Chris gave us the go-ahead."

"Okay, what's the plan?"

"You have to let them catch up and then freeze them. The problem is this: the icicles they've become will still be mobile. So, what you do is turn down the motors, and let them get in front of you. As soon as you do that, spin around and ice out their jets. We're on our way to keep them in check."

"And you're sure that's valid?"

"Not really." Rich did as John said, slowing down so that Brian and Team ABN could catch up with him.

"Haha! Is your old board wearing out on you Rich?"

"Yeah, I'm just no match for those things," Rich said with a hint of sarcasm.

"Top of the line, brand-new models by Natural Force. These boards could take you out any day of the week," Brian replied with a sneer.

"Well I hope they have fog protection," Rich said as he spread out the four engines and turned them on.

"Huh? That's not broken! There's nothing wrong with it," Brian's right-hand man, Jason exclaimed.

"Wow! You're right. You deserve a cookie, with Icing." Icing was the common Spaceball term for using a nitrogen engine to freeze other players. It was rarely performed; most people only did it during finals.

"I'll get you for this! Just as soon as my arms can move, I'll get you!"

"Oh no! Engine malfunctioning again," Rich said in a very serious voice. Once they were just past him, he turned on the engines in twin mode, which would use the two weaker engines to propel you forward, and the stronger engines to propel you backward; this was used for back-to-back Icing or Frosting. Frosting was the term for Icing someone's engines.

"Rich, now what are you doing? You're a strange little man," Brian said.

"Just Frosting your boards off," he replied as he hummed to himself.

"Icing *and* Frosting? That's low!"

"They don't call it the Abyss for nothing." Rich finally saw light up ahead, but he knew that he had to wait. He had three minutes left, this being the *first* timed game *ever*. Jordan and the others came down and kept the opponents under ice. However, the ref was about to come down, so Rich had to score after a short time.

Patrick Noble was relieved, because he didn't have to do any commentary. The producers of Spaceball Media, Inc. decided it took away from the sport. However, he was still sitting in the green section of the box seats, along with the other producers that favored the D^3 team. The problem with having no commentator is that Pat knew what was most likely happening, but he also knew most of the fans didn't have a clue.

Just as the ref entered the Abyss, Rich tossed the Spaceball into the room. The room was what many people had strived to see. He wasn't really that impressed; he had expected something bigger and better than just a green room. And that was all it was: a room that was completely green. "Hey Chris, you gotta check this place out," he said.

"On my way. John, Jordan, Bob, Rich found the end. He wants us to take a look at it." Everyone followed Chris to where Rich was waiting. "Whoa, what is?"

"It's the end of the road. This is where both of our Abysses end. You can see the tunnel right over there," Rich said as he pointed out a tunnel on the far wall.

"Okay boys, time to go," the ref told them. "There's really nothing to see here." They turned around and flew to the beginning of the Abyss.

"Ref, is that how all Abysses end?"

"Quite frankly John, I wouldn't know. That's the only Abyss they've allowed to go into, and that's just because we thought your radio connections were broken off. By the way, congrats on your second score. So far, this thing has been fairly one-sided."

"I think things are about to change. How much time do we have left, anyway?"

"Five minutes. Come on; they've thawed out by now," the ref said, indicating the other team.

"Not my fault they use combustion," Chris muttered. They flew to the very center of the spherical arena. The Spaceball shot up into Rich's hand, as he was the one who scored. Everyone watched as he hit it high into the air. It arced, which is exactly what Rich wanted. He and the rest of the team used the time to charge the other team. Four of them formed into a protective barrier, to let the fifth man catch the ball. As soon as the charging team came close, their opponents pulled a very unexpected move. Two of them shot downward, the other two going straight up, leaving the supposed receiver wide open to be hit. Chris and the team were going too fast to slant up or down, so they mobbed him, with the exception of John and Jordan, who turned around to counter the other team's move. They were on the outside, so maneuverability was easier for them.

"Didn't see that one coming," Rich told himself. He noticed that the turf had shown up. The fans had to watch on large HTVs until the turf was cleared. "Bob, Turf-X!"

"We don't have time; they're getting away!"

"Bob, I got him," Chris said. "You do the Turf-X. In fact, Jordan and John, pull off another one for me! We can see a whole lot better than them." Chris took off after the other team, which was far ahead of him. The rest of his team went to do the Twin Turf-X.

Team Alpha-Beta-Gnu turned back to see him catching up. Jeff, the captain, called for a Reversing V. This was a very difficult move, which involved setting up like ducks in a V formation, and then moving around to create a backwards V shape. The person at the rear would move to the front, the people in the front to the back, and the middle people would switch side-to-side. They did this over and over, passing the Spaceball from person to person, so that its position was always somewhat unknown.

Chris took off after them. His engines were evenly matched with theirs, so he had to find another way. He watched as John and Jordan performed their portion of the move on the ceiling. He knew that the only way to catch up was to confuse them with his baton. As soon as everyone else had finished the X move, they rejoined Chris, going at an angle.

"What's the plan?"

"You tell me," Chris replied to John. "Seriously, what I was thinking is this: they can't see at all. Neither can we. That means that we need to do something that we can do blindfolded that will really mess them up." Everyone knew what he meant. The other team had slowed down a lot, because they didn't ride with turfed space. They also slowed down because they thought Chris was further behind than he really was. He went full speed at them, wherever they were. He wasn't quite sure, but he knew they were going towards one of their two Abysses.

"Uh, Chris, how do we know which Abyss they're going to?"

"Jordan, you and Bob go to the bottom; you can still catch them, I hope. Everyone else, come with me."

"Oh, what's this? It appears as though I'm right at the edge of the Abyss. Should I? I don't know," Jeff taunted. He teetered on the edge, as if pondering the dangers of going down. Then, upon realizing that Jordan and Bob were following him at a more-than-healthy distance, he dropped the Spaceball, and it went straight in, scoring, in a very simple way.

Everyone returned to the center of the arena. All the Turf that was still attached to the walls was removed, but the orb in

It All Started In Chem Class...

which they played still had the dirt in it. The Spaceball came right to John. Due to their timely score, Team ABN had somewhere near four minutes left. John was in the middle of a five-man–free-for-all, the signature move of the team. Upon Bob's suggestion, the team moved into a D shape. The tactic worked fairly well, for a while.

Jeff and Brian knew what they had to do. It was a low blow, but such things went unsaid in Spaceball. Chris would never suspect. They each set up to run at someone to either side of Chris. As they closed in, they converged, so that each man would hit Chris at the exact same time. If they could break the D formation, they would deal a harsh blow, and the team would be one step closer to getting back the Spaceball.

"John, Rich, they're doing another run," Chris said, checking his rear view mirror, which came standard on his helmet.

"Yeah, I got him," Rich replied, dusting off his baton.

"Don't worry about us, Chris," John said confidently. They all turned back to the task that was at hand, playing out the free for all. None of them paid any attention to the people flying at them from behind. Chris was taken by surprise, and flipped around four or five times before he stopped. Even with his polyeurocarbonate armor, Chris had no idea what had happened. He was so dazed by the twin blow that he couldn't move. Brian and Jeff helped him, however, by moving him out of the way. They charged into the free for all, and got the Spaceball.

The other team had the Spaceball for the third time in the game. There were two and a half minutes left in regulation play. Although most games extended overtime, this would be a special extension. After two minutes, they were finally outside the Abyss. John and the others were in hot pursuit, with Chris still dazed and confused. With Chris temporarily out of commission, fending off their opponents was fairly easy, as they could double team one of them. However, they simply stood around in a circle, mocking their opponents. Upon realizing that there was only one minute left in the game, Jeff simply tossed it in, tying the game. This was the first Spaceball game with a time limit; a sudden death round could *not* decide the Spaceball champions of the world.

"Everyone, to the middle," the ref called out. "I have some very special rules that are going to be put into effect for the first time. They read, as drafted by the Commissioner of Spaceball, 'Should the game be tied with one minute or anything less remaining, these rules will be put into effect. Only two players from each team will be allowed to play in the overtime. You may choose any two people. Only the top and bottom Abysses will be used. I will throw the Spaceball, and the first person to catch it will have possession. If no one has scored at the end of five excessive minutes, we will have a second round with two more people playing. If necessary, a third round will be played with the remaining player.' Does everyone understand?"

"Yes," the teams replied in unison.

"Choose your first two players at this time."

"I'm playing," Jeff said.

"Me too," added another person from Jeff's team, named Aaron.

"John and Rich are playing for us," Chris, who was recovered, stated.

"Very well then, gentlemen, take your places over the colored platforms." They did as the ref said, and he withdrew a new Spaceball. It had their team colors, and looked very much like a Christmas ornament. "By the way, Rich, call it in the air."

"Heads," Rich said. It was. "Top," he said before the ref could even ask which goal he wanted. The Ref through the ball straight down, and it rebounded almost instantly. John sped into the air, neck and neck with Aaron. Aaron just barely got it first. He turned around and shoat towards the bottom of the arena. John, on the other hand, was set up to hit Aaron, and did just that. He slammed into him at full speed, despite attempts to prevent him by Jeff. Aaron had to speed back down after he spun around. Jeff sped out in front of him, to take the brunt of the attack attempted by Rich and John.

It All Started In Chem Class...

Aaron passed the ball to Jeff just as the firewall sprang up. While Rich and John tried to get it back from Jeff, Aaron went right into the center of the pit. Rich faked left, prompting the captain to throw the ball to Aaron, realizing only just too late that John had already anticipated that move.

John caught the ball and sped up towards his own goal. Rich flew behind him, trying to fend off attacks to protect him. The fans were going wild, but John wasn't really paying attention. Suddenly, turf began to fly at him from all directions. He was in a pitch-black environment.

Rich realized what his error was after seeing the effect it had. He let the other team get away; he didn't have much of a choice as they went in different directions. The turf had come out, and they used a very difficult two man maneuver called the turfball. A turfball was hard to form, but very effective if done correctly. They had to lift turf at just the right angle that it would form a large ball around the person with the Spaceball. The idea was to completely black-out the opponent. It worked especially well if the opponent in question didn't have a combustion engine.

John pushed on in some direction. He didn't know where he was or where he was going. He just knew that the only way to keep the ball was to keep moving. After a short time, however, that stopped working. He realized he was up against one of the walls. He used the motor on the Spaceball to get out. After he was out, he saw Rich trying to prevent the other team from getting to him, and it wasn't working very well. They had a head start, and John knew they were going to head him off at the Abyss. That was something he simply accepted, as he took off. He was at an angle to them, and soon he leveled out.

"Jeff! Turbo," Aaron called. They both understood the command, and kicked into the hyperdrive. They flew out to either side of John. Then, they slowly closed in, and finally hit him in a sandwich. It gave them an advantage, but John was still moving fast towards the Abyss.

"Nice try," John commented. "I'd expect no less, of course," he said mockingly. They spun around, right at the Abyss.

Rich was simply watching. He knew John could take them. *And besides,* he thought, *if we both go up there, there'll be no one to stop them on the rebound.*

John had seen a very risky move performed by Keno before. It was his signature move, the Asian Bullet. John was debating between that move and his own personal move, the Chemist. The Chemist was a very hard move to do, but also very successful. John had done it before, both right and wrong. He had never done it in such an important game, though. The Chemist could only be performed with the assistance of a Hydrogen tank. It was based on the basic Chemistry concept that Hydrogen was highly flammable in certain environments. John had a Hydrogen tank on the bottom of his board just for this move.

John brought the Spaceball down to near his engines. He neared the Abyss, but hid his own actions from the other team. He set the Spaceball right near his Nitro engine. The Spaceball was programmed to fly away from engines. That made John's plan even better. The minute he let go of the Spaceball, the Spaceball's engines went off, back-to-back with John's Hydrogen tank. The result was a huge explosion sending John flying immensely fast.

As he did, he saw Rich, who had somehow flown to the Abyss, also performing his personal move, the death spiral. He started low and spiraled up, closer and closer to his own Abyss. The Spaceball was caught in the fire, unable to escape. John moved faster than he ever had before, flying right at the other team. His speed alone scared them very badly; they flew out of the way, where Rich hit them in his normal spiraling path. They managed to overcome their fears and move back into John's path. John looked at his watch. He didn't know if he could pull it off in time.

Suddenly, the Abyss loomed in front of him, with Jeff and Aaron gripping each other's shoulder, despite their incredible fear. John would have moved, but he was going too fast to move. The minute he touched their arms, they dropped to their sides once more. He had a clear path to the bottom of the Abyss. The Spaceball was still powering him forward. Within seconds, he saw

It All Started In Chem Class...

the green room where the Spaceball must be placed. However, where it was there was a large sheet of some sort. He glanced back, and saw that Rich had continued his spiral into the Abyss itself. He waited until the spiral was just tight enough before continuing. John burst into the room, board still flaming, with Rich, leaving circular rings of Nitrogen behind him, coming in next.

John and Rich were both awestruck. They saw their entire team, from all the grades, the CEO of their sponsor, Satellite, Patrick Noble, and Wedgeheads all there to show support. John removed the Spaceball, which was now almost lifeless, and dropped it on the ground. As he received congratulations from his teammates, he realized that it was finally over. All the work and determination had paid off. And his board was free. *Man,* he thought, *I'm glad this is free.*

CHAPTER 21: FAREWELLS AND GOODBYES

"Nice job, John," Chris said, smiling. "Glad I put you in there. Rich, we couldn't have done it without you."

"Hey John," Bob told him. "You guys are going to have plenty of time to relax. By the way, we found out why the dean had the luxury ship built."

"Why?"

"So that we can ride home in style. He said he's taking off the speed controls. First, though, we got some publicity stuff to do."

"Do the reporters ever leave us alone?"

"Not when we win the first ever Spaceball championship on Planet X," Jordan replied. After telling the reporters how they did it and more useless details like that, they had to have a closed-door session with the CEO of Satellite. Upon entering the room

"What's up?"

"Well Chris, we're thinking about making Spaceball a year-round sport," the guy said. He paid Chris tons of money, and Chris still didn't know his name. "What do you guys think of that?"

"Ask me in six months," Jordan replied dryly.

"Give me a year or two to think," Rich answered.

"Sleep?" John looked around for a bed.

"I like that idea," Rich said.

"Maybe now's not a good time," the person answered with a laugh as he left.

Everyone changed back into regular clothes and boarded their shuttle home. With the speed control off, it didn't take long at all. In fact, it took less than a day at the speeds Chris took. Soon, they were back on the station, packing their bags for the trip back to Earth. Chris slept the entire way, as did most of his friends. He was greeted by his parents. They congratulated him

It All Started In Chem Class...

on the game, as did the giant crowd of Wedgeheads that were there to greet the team as the exited the shuttle. An entire year of college was over, and so was the greatest year of his life. But even after all of that, one thing still lingered in the back of his mind. He saw the dean, and ran over to see him.

"Hey Dean! I got a question for ya," Chris said to him.

"Shoot," the dean responded.

"Since you know about our encounter with the orb and all, what *was* that thing?"

"Orb? What orb?"